10103

Palo Alto City Library

The individual borrower is responsible for all library material borrowed on his or her card.

Charges as determined by the CITY OF PALO ALTO will be assessed for each overdue item.

Damaged or non-returned property will be billed to the individual borrower by the CITY OF PALO ALTO.

P.O. Box 10250, Palo Alto, CA 94303

HEAVENLY DAYS

ALSO BY JAMES WILCOX

Plain and Normal
Guest of a Sinner
Polite Sex
Sort of Rich
Miss Undine's Living Room
North Gladiola
Modern Baptists

HEAVENLY DAYS

a novel

James Wilcox

VIKING

VIKING
Published by the Penguin Group
Penguin Group (USA) Inc., 375 Hudson Street, New York, New York 10014, U.S.A.
Penguin Books Ltd, 80 Strand, London WC2R 0RL, England
Penguin Books Australia Ltd, 250 Camberwell Road, Camberwell, Victoria 3124, Australia
Penguin Books Canada Ltd, 10 Alcorn Avenue, Toronto, Ontario, Canada M4V 3B2
Penguin Books India (P) Ltd, 11 Community Centre, Panchsheel Park,
New Delhi – 110 017, India
Penguin Books (N.Z.) Ltd, Cnr Rosedale and Airborne Roads, Albany, Auckland, New Zealand
Penguin Books (South Africa) (Pty) Ltd, 24 Sturdee Avenue, Rosebank,
Johannesburg 2196, South Africa

Penguin Books Ltd, Registered Offices: 80 Strand, London WC2R 0RL, England

First published in 2003 by Viking Penguin, a member of Penguin Group (USA) Inc.

1   3   5   7   9   10   8   6   4   2

Copyright © James Wilcox, 2003
All rights reserved

PUBLISHER'S NOTE: This is a work of fiction. Names, characters, places, and incidents either are the product of the author's imagination or are used fictitiously, and any resemblance to actual persons, living or dead, business establishments, events, or locales is entirely co-incidental.

LIBRARY OF CONGRESS CATALOGING-IN-PUBLICATION DATA
Wilcox, James.
Heavenly days : a novel / James Wilcox.
p.   cm.
ISBN 0-670-03247-6
1. Tula Springs (La. : Imaginary place)—Fiction.   2. Women—Louisiana—Fiction.
3. Tax assessment—Fiction.   4. Bassoonists—Fiction.   5. Louisiana—Fiction.   I. Title.
PS3573.I396H43 2003
813'.54—dc21   2003050164

This book is printed on acid-free paper. ∞

Printed in the United States of America

Without limiting the rights under copyright reserved above, no part of this publication may be reproduced, stored in or introduced into a retrieval system, or transmitted, in any form or by any means (electronic, mechanical, photocopying, recording or otherwise), without the prior written permission of both the copyright owner and the above publisher of this book.

The scanning, uploading, and distribution of this book via the Internet or via any other means without the permission of the publisher is illegal and punishable by law. Please purchase only authorized electronic editions and do not participate in or encourage electronic piracy of copyrighted materials. Your support of the author's rights is appreciated.

To Rick
editor and friend
for over twenty years

Heaven, once attained, will work backwards and turn even that agony into a glory.

—C. S. LEWIS

CHAPTER ONE

On the third Tuesday of every month, Lou Jones sets the alarm for 4:30 A.M. so she can make it out to the toolshed by 5:15. There she allows herself exactly one hour and forty-five minutes to stitch together her column for the North American Bassoon Society newsletter. "Notes from Up and Down the Staff," it's called. To help her get this chore done, Lou's husband customized a plywood desk so that it curves around the riding lawnmower. Lou would have preferred to banish the lawnmower from the toolshed, but for tax purposes, she had to keep it there. A few weeks ago there had been some unpleasantness with City Hall. Because of the dimity curtains adorning the toolshed's bow window and the morning glories lacing its gutters, Mrs. Melvin Tudie, the newly elected tax assessor, decided that it was actually a guesthouse. Incensed, Lou's husband not only lugged the refrigerator out of the shed but also hauled off the daybed Lou needed to spread out her notes on the comings and goings of the Society's fully paid-up members.

Lou hoped that would be the end of it. But Don, her husband, was intent on making this into a federal case. The mayor himself would have to be informed that the air conditioning in the toolshed was absolutely essential for the financial records stored there, to keep off the goddam mildew. And the sink was only used to wash off gasoline and grease after mowing. As for the toilet, his wife had developed a slight bladder problem and needed one close by when she pruned her column. Luckily, the day before Don's appointment with the mayor, the tax assessor was admitted to the brand-new wing of the Pentecostal hospital for liposuction. Lou was able to convince Don to let sleeping dogs lie. And so far, no notice of an increase in property taxes has arrived in Lou's mailbox.

On this third Tuesday in September, Lou's having a particularly hard time with the column. When she types out all the news she's solicited, she's still 217 words short. After an arduous struggle, she ekes out the necessary words by grafting a few facts about how pink hydrangeas can be turned blue (sprinkle aluminum onto the soil) onto an item about a Waco bassoonist who tends a humming-bird garden. "Finito," Lou mutters as she stuffs the column into a priority mailer. Since the post office isn't open yet, she will leave the envelope with her husband on her way to work. He always promises to mail her column the minute the doors open. Before working out this system, Lou had been spending a small fortune on Federal Express. Needless to say, the Society never reimbursed her—not one red cent.

Lou's husband lives across town in a house owned by his parents. For health reasons, her in-laws have moved to a retirement com-munity in the Arizona desert. Lou had tried to sell their house for them, but every time a reasonable bid was made, Don's mother would get panicky and say how tired she was of water. (The retirees were living in a houseboat moored on an artificial lake.) If some-thing should ever happen to Don Sr., God forbid, well then, she would probably want to move back to dry land. Lou then suggested renting the house. There was a friend of a friend at work who would be willing to take it on a month-to-month basis. With a sigh,

Lou's mother-in-law agreed to the proposal, as long as the new tenant didn't change a stick of furniture in the house.

Lou saved her in-laws so much money by fixing the leaky faucets and stopped-up toilets herself that, even if Don grumbled about her overalls, she felt a surge of something with the accomplishment—most likely, self-esteem. The rent, though, was another matter. After it hadn't been paid for three months in a row, the friend of a friend started filling up the house with boarders. A librarian and a U-Haul mechanic took up residence in the den, while the north and west bedrooms were occupied by nail sculptors. When the neighbors started complaining about the noise from an endlessly repeated *Titanic* soundtrack, Lou offered to help the illegal subtenants find nice, cheap efficiency apartments. The sculptors took her up on this, but the librarian and the mechanic claimed they were not illegal. In fact, they told Lou she had better quit her snooping around—peeling Popeye's chicken skin from the linoleum, vacuuming, setting out roach motels, this was what they called "snooping"—or they'd swear out a complaint for trespassing.

If it weren't for Don, the house on Coffee Ridge Road would probably still be under siege. Lou, of course, could not approve of her husband's tactics. She herself had been planning legal redress through a talented arbitrator who cleaned their pool and threw clay pots. But before Lou could map out a strategy with the potter, Don barreled over to his parents' house and cleared out all the squatters' belongings, tossing them right out onto the carport after a brief altercation with the librarian, a fistfight the details of which Lou really didn't want to hear about. To make sure that the librarian didn't carry out his threat to return with Martha Stewart wallpaper for the den, Don had all the locks changed and then installed himself in the east bedroom.

He's been standing guard there now for about six weeks or so, during which time Lou's noticed a definite improvement in their marital relations. For some reason, with a house of his own, Don seems more attentive and courteous. He no longer suspects her of using his toothbrush or leaving rings on the coffee table. As for Lou, she's free to eat exactly what she wants—and when. And she can sleep on her plain white polyester sheets, cheap and easy to wash. No more looks from the dry cleaner when she brings in the black satin ones Don favors.

"Knock, knock," Lou calls out as she unlocks the back door of her in-laws'. "Just me—don't shoot."

Not long ago, Lou entered the premises without announcing herself and was greeted by an alarming bark—in what sounded like Korean or something. This Don bellowed out in a crouch, ready to spring. Apparently, he still hadn't recovered from the contretemps with the librarian, but Lou was not persuaded that buying a $59.95 tae kwon do videotape was the best way to go about restoring one's peace of mind. Tai chi was what she had recommended, the *free* classes they were offering senior citizens at the new recreation center. Don protested that being fifty didn't qualify him as a senior citizen, and Lou had to agree that it was hard to imagine him as a senior anything, the way he behaved sometimes.

Don looks up from the base of the food pyramid he's working on—a bowl heaped with oat-bran dinosaurs. *Does one really need six to eleven servings of grains and bread per day?* Lou wonders. If she ate as much as these cereal boxes advised, she would have time for nothing else. And yet it's Don who never gains an ounce. She, who rarely slows down for a square meal, weighs almost as much as the librarian's girlfriend, the U-Haul mechanic. The librarian himself, though, is so willowy that it's no wonder Don was caught off guard by his left hook. A real gentleman, Don just protected his face, never really punching the diminutive young man back very hard, and finally steered him out the door with a hammerlock.

"No, thanks," she says to the green banana he's waggling in her face. "I don't have time. Here's the column, dear. Will you promise to get it there first thing? And don't let Mr. Singhmarishi tell you he's out of receipts again. I want a receipt."

Propping the envelope against a guava, Lou sniffs the air. He's been at it again, cleaning every surface in the kitchen, from the island he's hunched over to the pewter cows with nutmeg and cumin in their bellies. Pine cleaner, ammonia, Lysol—all these telltale scents not quite masked by a heavy dose of lilac air freshener. This is what Don does when he can't sleep. The smell would always wake Lou at three or four in the morning, back before Don moved to Coffee Ridge. Well, she supposes it's a harmless enough outlet. Being downsized can't be a very pleasant experience for anyone. But for Don, who's always been so responsible, such a dedicated employee, it was a crushing blow. What a good provider he's been, too—buying her that lavish showplace they can't afford now, ignoring her pleas for a more modest home without all the track lighting and alarms that make her feel like a live-in docent.

"What, Lou? Why are you staring at me?"

"I was just thinking what a handsome man I've got."

"Got where?"

Even though Don's not conventionally handsome, Lou began to realize shortly after he moved out to guard his parents' property, after he wasn't constantly underfoot, day in day out, that her husband was really not bad-looking at all, not by a long shot. For a fifty-year-old he's in great shape—lean and mean and only an inch or two shorter than she would normally prefer. If only he would let his hair grow out. That crew cut makes him look like a drill sergeant, if drill sergeants dyed their hair. That's another thing she'd appreciate, if he'd throw out the Grecian Formula and just let it be, his hair. She's not ashamed of *her* gray. If anything, it's a badge of honor.

She's digging in her purse for the keys to the BMW when she notices the rubber band around her wrist. Something important she must remember. What is it? Oh, yes. "That printer, Don. It's still cluttering up my desk. You promised me a week ago you'd give it back to Alpha."

Alpha is another luxury they can ill afford, what with Don still looking for work. But even when they were flush, Lou never felt comfortable with the idea of having a housekeeper. She only gives Alpha the lightest chores and does the real work herself. Maybelle,

Don's mother, was behind all this. For years Alpha had worked for Don's parents, and when they moved to Arizona, Maybelle made her son promise to hire the woman. Lou protested, of course, insisting that Alpha deserved a job with more dignity—and decided to pay for her education. Alpha, though, tore up Lou's check. She did not accept handouts from anyone. Since she was sixteen, Alpha has been on her own, working her way from Mombasa to Freetown, from Grenada to Tula Springs. Just what sort of education did Lou think she needed after all she, Alpha, had been through? *Please do not speak to me about* dignity, *Lou Jones.*

With a paper towel Don wipes up a few drops of lactose-free milk. "It's going to hurt her feelings, Lou."

"How can she afford to give me a birthday present like that?"

"Printers aren't that expensive, babe. Besides, I might have helped out a little myself."

Even after all these years of being married to him, Lou can hardly believe her ears. How often has she told him she doesn't want a computer? And where in heaven's name did he think she would find the time to learn how to use one? Why, she doesn't even have a spare minute to play the $17,000 bassoon he gave her back in 1987, after the bunion surgery. It's been months, years, since she's touched the darn thing.

"All right, that's it." Lou pats the Formica counter blindly, hoping she will perhaps *feel* the keys she has lost. "You take that printer back today, J. Donald Jones."

"I thought if you saw how small it was, you wouldn't be afraid of the rest. A laptop hardly takes up any space at all."

With the back of her hand, she swipes at a tear. "You want to send us to the poorhouse, is that it? Don't *sssh* me."

Alpha's mother's bedroom is right off the kitchen, and Don's been reminding her of this with a finger to his lip or pointing to the door.

"Keep it down, Lou."

"No, I won't be shushed in my own—in a home I unclogged on my hands and knees when everyone knows there are certain things female tenants should never flush down the toilet. And what thanks do I get? Does your mother realize what a real plumber would cost her?"

"Mrs. Ompala," Don warns, nodding again toward the bedroom door.

Recently widowed, Alpha's mother had booked passage on a freighter from Mombasa to visit her daughter. But it seems Alpha's studio in the Hollywood Apartments just wasn't meant to house two adults without a certain amount of friction. While Alpha searches for more suitable quarters, Mrs. Ompala is making do at Don's parents'. She would much rather have checked into a hotel, but Don has insisted she be his guest at Coffee Ridge. Besides, Tula Springs doesn't have a hotel—just a Super8 with video poker in every room, and it lies three miles outside the city limits.

Lou has had only one encounter with Alpha's mother, an unfortunate one just a couple of days ago. It was so thoughtless of Don not to have told her that unlike her daughter, Mrs. Ompala isn't African-American—or rather, whatever . . . Lou covered her initial confusion with a too-hearty welcome, which Mrs. Ompala, a pale, regal woman of uncertain age, returned with a dim smile. Never had Lou been confronted by such elegance, such style. Every gesture of Mrs. Ompala's, every syllable she uttered betrayed a breeding, a restraint that made the stains on Lou's overalls loom like a veritable map of ignorance and squalor. And the woman's outfit, the way her immaculate cotton dress was draped so perfectly, every fold as graceful as a pietà's—well, is it any wonder that Lou tried to work into the conversation a casual mention of her Ph.D., the way she dissected the Lydian mode in *Verklärte Nacht*?

"You looking for these?" Don shoves Lou's keys across the island. Somehow they had wound up behind a porcelain cow oozing honey.

As she licks the BMW keys clean, he says, "You know she's expecting you for tea this afternoon."

"What, I'm supposed to drop everything because her ladyship wants tea?" she grumbles, delighted. She is to have another chance, after all. This time will be different. No mention of her Ph.D. And most certainly, no overalls.

"At five. You're home by then, Lou."

"No, it's impossible. I've got to transcribe those minutes, you know, and pick up . . ."

"For me, babe—come on. Do it for me."

The way his voice cracks, slightly hoarse, is just how the sophomore manager of the baseball team had sounded when he tried, and failed, to act casual with the head cheerleader, herself, a senior. To be adored like that, worshiped with a hopeless love—yes, that element of despair was so oddly appealing that she finally couldn't resist. It triggered in her a curious, blind adoration in return.

"And don't let Mr. Singhmarishi bully you," she says on her way out. "You have a perfect right to get a receipt in the post office."

"Shhh! Mrs. Ompala."

CHAPTER TWO

Because the space reserved for Lou's BMW is occupied she has no choice but to park in the handicapped zone. It's either that or drive across the railroad tracks and squeeze in front of the Feed and Seed, then trudge back through those sunflowers where the waitperson at the Bulgar Barbeque Service Two got bit by a deer tick and emigrated back to her native Mississippi. Lou's been to her town, Burdin, once to deliver an address on the family of wind instruments. This meant the lunch she had eaten at the Bulgar Service One way up there in north Mississippi could be a legitimate deduction, as could the pantsuit she wore to lecture in. Next door to the Bulgar Service in Mississippi was a Lane Bryant, where she bought another pantsuit—charcoal with off-white piping. The off-white bothered her, though, as it made the suit look as if it hadn't been properly cleaned. She probably wouldn't have bought the outfit at all if the goat she had sampled at the Bulgar buffet hadn't necessitated the use of a restroom—and the department store's was so much more trustworthy. She doesn't believe it's right to use a store's accommodations without being a legitimate customer—and besides, the suit was 30 percent off.

It's this very suit, the charcoal, that Lou has on as she hurries into the defunct railroad station that's been tastefully renovated into Tula Springs' prime office space. Layers of green paint have been stripped from the carved oak doors to reveal intricate whorls and boles that Lou admires every time she slides her ID card into the STAFF ONLY slot. She even feels a little house-proud. Once a week she rubs an expensive preservative she's yet to be reimbursed for onto the panels.

Although there's no written guideline on the matter, Lou knows that the director of WaistWatch frowns on the consumption of bagels at one's desk. But the chocolate bagel in her drawer is about to expire, the wrapper warns. And besides, all she had for supper last night was a WaistWatchChocoLite mousse.

After checking to make sure that Brother Moodie, the director of the makeover franchise, is discipling his 7:10 A.M. aerobics class, Lou nibbles discreetly at the receptionist's desk. From time to time she can't help glancing down at the piping on her suit. These glances make her more and more unhappy. Finally, she resolves to do something about it. She will have to swallow her pride and ask Maigrite to cover for her.

Maigrite is the friend whose friend double-crossed Lou by turning her in-laws' into a boardinghouse. Most people regard Maigrite as cold and standoffish, a snob. But Lou is an expert at bringing out the best in some of the most difficult individuals on earth. It wasn't for nothing that Anya Magda-Louise Vogelsanger had been elected Sweetheart of a fraternity renowned for its lively parties. Two brothers, in fact, had been jailed for battery and assault, another for armed robbery. In any case, Lou genuinely does like Maigrite and is content to let bygones be bygones. It isn't Maigrite's fault that her friend has absolutely no conscience.

After hiding the bagel wrapper and sweeping the jimmies off her desk, Lou strolls over to Maigrite's module by the rubber plant strung with festive lights. (*Every day at WaistWatch is Christmas*, the franchise's orientation booklet explains. *Every client is gifted every day with a rise in self-esteem.*) Except for business matters—the phone calls Lou fields at the reception desk—she and Maigrite haven't exchanged a word in two, maybe three, days. It's always the bigger person, Lou knows, who must break the ice.

"That collar is so lovely," Lou ventures bravely. Whether it's fear or love that's making her heart pound so violently, Lou isn't sure. Maigrite has always inspired an equal amount of both in her. The love started out as pity for Maigrite's frail, childlike arms, so thin she has to wear a sweater even in the hottest months. Today's angora has a fur collar attached with Diamonette clips. "Ermine seems like such an original touch—for September."

After an unsettling silence, during which Maigrite juggles a formidable array of windows on her screen, Lou hears, "It's Belgian hare."

As Maigrite cascades the windows, Lou admires the woman's silky olive skin and the distinctive nose. Although she looks Cajun, Maigrite's a First Baptist from Liberty, where you won't find a single Catholic, she claims.

"What is it, Louise? I'm busy, can't you see?"

"Nothing, really. It's just that, well, I really don't mind your parking in my reserved space right on top of my name, but . . ."

"You want me to use the handicapped space—is that it?"

As a result of a childhood fever, one of Maigrite's legs is shorter than the other. Maigrite had first shared this information with Lou in a brusque, matter-of-fact way when Lou invited her to lunch at the Bulgar buffet. That was almost a year ago, and Maigrite still hasn't got her own designated parking space in front of WaistWatch.

"Have you spoken to Lynda? You really have to be firm with the woman, Maigrite. Keep at her. She's very forgetful."

Long ago, Lynda, Maigrite's boss, promised to convert the handicapped space into a personal space for Maigrite. After all, there are no handicapped personnel working in the defunct train station.

"I told you, Lou—I never park in handicapped, ever."

"But it won't be handicapped anymore if they paint your name over it."

"It's still blue. Everyone else has white lines."

"Well, that's no problem. I'll buy the white paint myself. In fact, I could get some this afternoon if you'll cover for me. I need to leave at three-thirty."

Maigrite pats the sequined net holding her chignon in place. "Skipping out again?"

Lou can't help resenting that "again." When has she ever skipped out? Last week she was compelled to drive Don to a job interview in Ozone because the bonnets on his axles had worn out. And the new prescription eyedrops he was supposed to use before going to bed, not in the morning, had made the world one big blur for him. It was such an important interview, too: $168,000 the job would have paid—software program director at Lantana BuyProducts. In a way, though, she was glad he'd been turned down. Could a man who'd earned himself not one, but two Ph.D.'s—in plant pathology and computer engineering—really have found happiness recycling petroleum sludge into waterproof mascara? He deserved better.

"Maigrite, it happens to be a medical . . . need."

Lou is not going to let Mrs. Ompala see her in this piping. If she leaves by 3:30, she'll have time to steam out the wrinkles in the Valentino cocktail frock Don bought her for one of his boss's dinner parties. Then she would see if Hulga at the beauty college could do an emergency job on her perm, touch it up a bit. It's frizzing so bad now, unable to stand a chance against all this humidity.

"Just a minute," Maigrite says, picking up the phone that hasn't rung. WaistWatch has installed vibrators in the staff's chairs to signal incoming calls so clients will not be distracted by undue noise. It's taken Lou a while to get used to this. In fact, at first it was so unsettling, this tingling in her loins, that she seriously considered quitting. But WaistWatch is the only job in town that doesn't require computer literacy for its receptionist. In fact, she is forbidden to touch any computers at work. Whether this has something to do with her refusal to let Brother Moodie rebirth her, she isn't sure. She herself, of course, doesn't endorse the prevailing religious sensibility at work. As an Episcopalian, Lou has many reservations about the way the Lord's name is bandied about during office hours. There's something vaguely unbecoming about shedding pounds for Jesus or letting Jesus throw out your old wardrobe.

Aside from this, though, and the little difficulty with Maigrite, the work environment couldn't be more pleasant. No one's ever discriminated against Lou for being Episcopalian. And Lynda, Maigrite's boss, has even stopped pestering her to take advantage of the employee discount for ScriptureSpinning. Lou hasn't the slightest desire to virtually bike through HolyLand.

Maigrite hangs up. "That man . . ." Sighing, she dabs her temples with the toilet water kept specially on hand for her migraines.

"Your husband?" This, of course, is rhetorical. Maigrite always dabs after speaking to Mr. Pickens. "Please give him my best. Don and I have been meaning to have you and Mr. Pickens over for dinner just as soon as I get some time to . . ."

"If you think that the superintendent would set himself down at the same table with a man who started up a fistfight with a woman half his age . . . It's just a miracle y'all weren't sued from here to next Sunday."

"Oh, no, Maigrite. It wasn't the young woman, the U-Haul. It was her boyfriend, that's who Don started the fight with—I mean, *didn't* start the fight with."

"What young man?"

"The librarian, he was the one who attacked poor Don. Why, it's made him nervous as a cat."

With deft precision, Maigrite wields an emery board over her sculpted nails, not even glancing down once. "Girl, you putting me on? Grant isn't a man."

"Oh my . . . I thought with that crew cut, so brisk, you know. And those nice trousers . . . Though I did have my doubts about his . . . Well, he wasn't very manly, I admit. But why in heaven's name must she call herself Grant? That really isn't fair. Don and I never knew what to think about him."

"Don't play Miss Innocent with me. You know your stock soared here because of that fistfight. And Grant's her last name. Tammie Faye Grant."

Lou blinks. "Oh, I see. But what do you mean, my 'stock soared'?"

"Lynda's saying how maybe you Sunday golfers aren't such heathens after all. Had the gumption to show those sodomites the door—and give them a taste of the good Lord's vengeance."

Lou feels a curious tingling, as if she should pick up a phone. "Oh, Maigrite, this is awful. I feel like two cents."

"Y'all really thought she was a man?"

"I swear." Lou crosses her heart. "I remember thinking to myself, *this poor boy can't really like women that much.* That's why Don refused to hit him back. My husband is a gentleman, Maigrite. That's one thing you can count on."

Not really sure if she and Maigrite have made up or not, Lou hurries off to the changing room, where there's a beige toilet that she's twice unclogged. Both times Lynda mailed her a handwritten thank-you note. This gesture really made Lou feel appreciated, even if she could have done without the mauve cross on the scented Care Bears stationery.

CHAPTER THREE

It costs a fortune to have the Valentino dry-cleaned, and since Lou's worn it only once since the last cleaning she thought she could get away with steaming it herself this time. But the minute she walks in the Coffee Ridge house, she knows it was a mistake. Mrs. Ompala's eyes go right to the dress. And the woman can tell—oh, yes, Lou's sure she can tell—that the crimson frock wasn't properly cleaned. In fact, as Lou airs her views on Maigrite, saying how she suspects that the poor thing might be anorexic and should seek help, she notices a grease stain on the taffeta flounce. So she balances a coaster on her knee, right over the spot made long ago by Don's former boss's aunt's corn dog.

"No, Mrs. Ompala, not the painter—this is a woman, Maigrite Pickens. She works with my wife." Don speaks distinctly, as if he's translating for Lou, who's already explained who Maigrite is.

"Your wife?"

Don nods toward Lou.

"Oh, such a lovely woman," Mrs. Ompala comments, as if Lou, planted somewhat uncertainly in a listing rocker that squeaks every time she tries not to move, were elsewhere, in another room. The spotless panes of the sunporch seem to magnify the rays aimed at her. Virtually blinded, Lou has made an attempt to sit

next to Don, but was urged by a vigorous shake of his head not to
disturb the seating arrangement that was established when she arrived, twenty minutes late. And she has also been dissuaded from
helping herself to tea, for Mrs. Ompala is pouring. And no, Don explained, Mrs. Ompala would not prefer talking in the living room,
where it would be cooler. Mrs. Ompala always takes her tea in the
conservatory.

"Conservatory!" Lou will say to her husband after Mrs. Ompala
has retired for the evening. "Why must you talk such nonsense,
Don? It's a sunporch with a wilted ficus and a hot-water heater
sticking out like a sore thumb."

"I can't help how she talks."

"Fine, but you don't have to go aping her, talking about me in
the third person . . ."

"It's actually not a ficus."

"As if I were already a fond memory." Lou rather enjoys this
grumbling. She doesn't know why, but Mrs. Ompala made her feel
much younger, more alive. To be patronized by such a woman was
better, far better, than being flattered by the routine praise of Lou's
many friends. Indeed, Mrs. Ompala has the ability to make her
slights seem somewhat charming, almost endearing. It wasn't so
much what the woman said—in black and white, surely her words
would look petty, mean-spirited. But the way she delivered her
lines, the peculiar lilt—well, Lou can't seem to get enough of it.
She will rehash the tea as much as her husband can stand it.

"And for the life of me, J. Donald Jones, why did you have to
bring up that Nazi business?"

"What? I never . . ."

She distinctly remembers his very words. Lou's father was a
Kraut, he said.

"A what?" Mrs. Ompala asked.

"When he first came here to Tula Springs, everyone suspected
him, thought he was a Nazi because of his accent."

Sheathed in pearl-gray silk, Mrs. Ompala glanced in the general direction of the rocker, where Lou's crimson ruffles lan-
guished like a WinnDixie hibiscus still unsold after a fortnight.

"How interesting," Mrs. Ompala commented as she refreshed Lou's teacup. They were not drinking from Don's parents' Green Stamps china. Don had gone home and retrieved the Sèvres she never used—not even for company. For him to have paid so much for china was a downright sin. They had to keep it locked up in the Wallace Nutting whatnot wired with a display light and an alarm, which accidentally went off once when Lou was spraying NoWax polish. Mrs. Melvin Tudie had responded to the alarm. This was before the woman was elected tax assessor, when her only job was running the private security company that patrolled Lou's gated neighborhood.

"The Jews, of course," Mrs. Ompala said. Or something like that. Lou shaded her eyes while waiting for her to go on. But that seemed to be it.

"And you just sat there," Lou comments later while Don applies a chamois to the Sèvres roses. "You didn't even tell her my mother's Jewish."

"No, and I didn't tell her my mother's Baptist, either. Besides, she didn't say anything derogatory. You're too sensitive, Lou."

But it sounded wrong, what Mrs. Ompala had said. Was she implying that it was only the Jews in Tula Springs who suspected Lou's father? For her information, the only Jew in Tula Springs at that time was her mother, period, who was somehow, in a way Lou has never been able to fathom, a direct descendant of Jefferson Davis and, more vaguely, a certain Trotsky who had never lived in Mexico.

"My father was a very devout Catholic," Lou tried to explain. "He had to flee from Bavaria after he refused to serve in the German army."

"An R.C.?" Mrs. Ompala's gray eyes roved wistfully to the ficus-like plant. "Your wife is a papist?"

"Episcopalian," Don said. "We go to Frederik Memorial."

"Do they have evensong? I do miss my evensong. It regulates one's life so nicely. The chapel at Magdalen, just before sunset . . ." Mrs. Ompala completed the sentence with a sip of the Lapsang Souchong, her one and only sip of the evening. Any more than that, this sip seemed to imply, would be vulgar. "The bishop preached there once, my uncle. We used to have such fun at the palace. Lady Fitzhoward let me dance with her goat. Does your wife enjoy goats, Jones?"

"No, I don't believe she does."

"Don, when did I ever say I don't enjoy goats?"

"What about that goat you ate in Mississippi? I never heard the end of it. She had to lecture these hyperactive kids, see, and my wife's plumbing, well, it's not exactly top of the line. One prune and, brother, need I say more?"

The horror on Mrs. Ompala's face was written in the most delicate cursive. As Don did indeed go on to say more about Lou's sensitive constitution, Lou raised her voice a few notches: "I was lecturing way up in north Mississippi, Mrs. Ompala—Burdin. They have this wonderful restaurant there, Bulgar, and I suppose because of my doctorate, someone on the Humanities Council contacted me to—quiet, Don sweetie, I can't hear myself think. My dissertation was on Schoenberg, his use of the Lydian mode in . . ."

"Burdin?" Mrs. Ompala mused. The hot-water heater shuddered. "Do they award doctorates there?"

"Oh, no, there's no college in Burdin. My degree is from Florida State, it's one of the premier music schools in the country. It was just ranked by *U.S. News and*—help me out, Don, and what? Anyway, ahead of Yale, Princeton, and Harvard. That's where I got my doctorate."

"Oh, yes, Harvard—in what they call Cambridge, I believe."

Lou smiled ruefully. "Not the *real* Cambridge, of course. Cookie?"

"I don't eat biscuits, Dr. Jones. Thank you."

CHAPTER FOUR

Lou discovers quickly that it really isn't easy to paint over blue. Her brush teaches her that asphalt is not as smooth as it seems, its pits and humps ruining her straight line. From time to time Maigrite deigns to stir the ivory paint Lou purchased across the railroad tracks at the bargain store. But does the woman offer to lift a finger to actually help paint? No, she's just perched there on the fender of Lynda's Cougar with the plastic stirrer in one hand and a WWLite KiwiJava in the other.

"I never told her I went to Harvard," Lou says as she plucks a tung leaf off the blue line. "Don was right there. He heard me say Florida State."

"So what's the big deal?" Maigrite kicks at a dragonfly that's landed on Lou's meatloaf, her lunch.

"I just don't need Don correcting me. Telling her I hadn't gone to Harvard when I never said . . . Anyway, I shouldn't have got this at Sonny Boy, this paint. It's so thin, hardly covers a thing."

"I wish you'd stop calling it Sonny Boy, Lou. It's Freds been Freds for ages."

All her life the store's been Sonny Boy, except for the last couple of years—hardly ages. Lou finds it depressing, so many places changing names. Like when JoJo's Poboys suddenly became Bulgarian.

With a grip on the Cougar's fender, Lou pulls herself up off her knees, both of which ache something fierce. "I'm going to have to go to Wal-Mart and get some decent paint, Maigrite. This stuff just isn't covering the blue."

"I've always said it doesn't pay to cut corners."

Taking a bite of the cold meatloaf, Lou lets this pass. The real reason she went to Sonny Boy—Freds—was not because the paint might be cheaper. It was mainly an excuse to see the manager, Maigrite's friend, the one who had initially rented her in-laws' house. Lou felt obliged to explain to Mrs. Van Buren that her husband, Don, was not prejudiced against women who preferred women. As a matter of fact, Don liked them so much that he had been expelled from The Citadel for secreting a picture of a young lady kissing another young lady in his gym shorts. (Lou, of course, was not going to mention this incident to Mrs. Van Buren. It was something she herself was trying hard to forget.)

After paying for the quart of paint, Lou had strolled back to the manager's office. Although the clerk had assured her it would be all right to just walk right in, Lou was not that sort of person. She always knocked first. When no one answered, she had second thoughts about the whole thing. Why was it necessary to explain her lack of prejudice to a woman who had tried to turn a fast buck by illegally subletting Don's parents' house? Lou really wished she could stop herself from wanting everyone to like her. She had read somewhere that this wasn't healthy, that it was more normal to have a lot of people think you were rotten.

As she turned to leave, the door opened, and there stood Maigrite's husband, Mr. Pickens. A little disconcerted, Lou asked if Mrs. Van Buren might possibly have a moment to chat. Mr. Pickens, who always looked so innocent—far too innocent, actually, as if he had never done a thing in his life—informed her that Burma wasn't there, that she had gone out for a latte break, and that he himself was extremely busy and had to get back to a deposition he was taking, very important. Lou apologized again and said how it looked as if he had lost some weight. Mr. Pickens said two pounds—and with no thank-you, no good-bye, shut the door.

Lugging the can of paint around the hairy stems of the sunflowers, Lou wondered if Mr. Pickens had been rude to her. He had virtually slammed the door in her face. And how could he be taking a deposition if no one was in the office? He wasn't a lawyer, anyway, but had just been a paralegal once. Were superintendents of streets, parks, and garbage somehow empowered to take depositions? Was that possible?

While she was painting over the stylized blue wheelchair on the asphalt and trying to make sense of Don's unfair remark about Harvard, Lou was also pondering whether she should mention to Maigrite that she had seen her husband at the bargain store. Could it be that the deposition had something to do with Mrs. Van Buren's eviction? Was Burma Van Buren going to make trouble? It would be so terribly ungrateful if Mr. Pickens got himself mixed up in legal proceedings. Did he have no memory at all? Mr. Pickens owed his job to her. When he ran for superintendent of streets, parks, and garbage last year, she cast her vote for him because Maigrite assured her he hadn't the slightest chance of winning. And Lou had encouraged Don to vote for him, too, since Mr. Pickens's self-esteem needed bolstering after he was blackballed by the Hair Club for Men. Wouldn't you know, Mr. Pickens won, beating out Olive Mackie, the Democrat, by a single chad.

And here she was being corrected again. Freds, she was saying, this woman who had once asked Lou what Phi Beta Kappa meant. Yes, it had been Maigrite who had interviewed Lou for the job at WaistWatch, Maigrite who had required twelve copies of Lou's resumé for the corporate headquarters in Nassau. If only Maigrite could have been there when Mrs. Ompala finally spoke directly to her—and called her *Dr.* Jones. Students used to call her that—Dr. Jones—back when she was teaching theory at St. Jude Community College, making $6,500 a year—slave labor, really—for a 5/5 load. But none of those students ever made those three syllables sound the way Mrs. Ompala had. Lou prickled all over, so coarse was her delight. And before retiring to her quarters, Mrs. Ompala had repeated them again. "I bid you a pleasant evening, Dr. Jones."

Lou's resentment never lasts for long. Trailing her boss into the remodeled train station, she tries not to notice the limp, the Olive Oyl legs. But her heart is wrung. In the noonday sun, Maigrite's spangled mohair shimmers, brazen as a Mardi Gras float.

"You know I mean it," Lou says as she scoots ahead to card open the door for Maigrite. "I really want you and Mr. Pickens to come over for dinner, soon as I have a free evening. Alpha makes the most delicious curries. Of course, they nearly wreck my system, so spicy, you know. But if I have company and don't ask Alpha to cook—well, I tried it once with my Gourmet Club, and she didn't speak to me for a whole week. Thought I was ashamed of her cooking."

Lou wishes there were a way to do the cooking herself. If Alpha was around, she, Alpha, might say something to Maigrite about the other house, how Don was still living there. And then Maigrite would most likely think that Lou and Don were overreacting to the illegal subtenants, that the house didn't really need protecting. Maigrite might even get the idea that Lou and Don weren't getting along as well as they should. How ironic that would be. Lou's never liked Don better than in these past few weeks of freedom. Her love, of course, has always been constant, unwavering. But love, she's learned, is mostly hard work, sacrifice. It's *liking* she's missed, the frosting on the cake. And now that she finally likes her husband, genuinely enjoys his company, she doesn't need anyone making her doubt the propriety of the situation. It reminds her of the days before she and Don were married, when they *did* live together, and everyone tried to make them think it was so wrong.

At her desk that afternoon, Lou is highlighting a sentence in Susan Brownmiller, a reference to Kate Millet, when her loins begin to tingle. Closing the book, she reaches for the phone. "Waist-Watch speaking. How may we service you today?"

It's Maigrite calling from the other end of the room. She says she just got an e-mail from Mrs. Melvin Tudie. The tax assessor is on her way over from City Hall to inspect their parking lot. "You shouldn't have tried to paint it over, Lou."

"Must that woman poke her nose into everyone's business?"

"It wasn't her. It was the superintendent. He rode by and saw the white paint over the blue. He wants Mrs. Tudie to find out who did it. If I were you, Lou, I'd hide that paint."

"I most certainly will not. I've done nothing wrong."

Nevertheless, Lou does move the can of ivory from her desk to a spot behind the festooned rubber plant.

CHAPTER FIVE

W hen the mauve light over the door flashes, Lou's prepared to stand her ground. She's not going to be intimi-
dated in this case just because her toolshed might be
reassessed. The parking lot is private property, after all. The city
doesn't have any right to tell an offshore corporation how they
must divide up their parking spaces. Or does it? In any case, the
tax assessor is a parish office. Mrs. Tudie has no business taking up
space in City Hall when she should be in the courthouse in Ozone.
Of course, she's officially listed with a courthouse address, which
she occupies in cyberspace to avoid the thirty-mile commute.

Smiling bravely, Lou deactivates the lock from the color code
bar on her desk console. The oak doors motor open and there
stands, clutching her purse, not Mrs. Melvin Tudie, but Mrs. Van
Buren, looking a little lost, as most people do when they first enter
WaistWatch. It takes a while to adjust to the dim flesh tones that
bathe the interior in a Lamaze-like womb.

Blinking rapidly, Mrs. Van Buren takes a couple of steps in the
wrong direction before veering correctly toward the reception
desk. "Lou, is that you?"

"Yes, hon. C'est moi." Lou hands her a tissue from the designer box she keeps handy. People's eyes tend to water if the contrast is too great between outside and inside WaistWatch.

Mrs. Van Buren dabs. "You wanted to see me? Oh, Lou . . ." Mrs. Van Buren's shapely hand stretches forth to finger a pearl on one of Lou's unpierced lobes.

"Don got them at Saks, Burma. In New Orleans. I wish he hadn't. I'm sure I'm going to lose them someday."

Mrs. Van Buren's eyes blur with admiration. Lou has a sudden urge to unscrew them, these earrings that are too expensive for everyday use, that she must nonetheless wear to prevent Don's feelings from being hurt, and hand them over. It would be crazy, of course. Mrs. Van Buren is her enemy, the thoughtless ex-tenant who made Don take up tae kwon do. And yet, every time Lou tries to get the woman to see how wrong she was, how unjust it was not to pay the rent month after month, how illegal it was to sublet the house without permission, on every one of these visits to give Mrs. Van Buren a piece of her mind, Lou finds herself liking the woman more and more.

"Lou, I've got a confession," Mrs. Van Buren says after refusing to accept the earrings as a gift. Lou, apparently, could not resist that urge. "I wasn't getting some latte. I was in the office all the time—under the desk. He made me get there, Mr. Pickens did. All my clothes were on, Lou—cross my heart, so help me God. We weren't doing a thing wrong, I swear."

Glancing over her shoulder, Lou hopes Maigrite can't hear any of this. The last thing Lou needs now is to get embroiled in Maigrite's domestic concerns.

"And, Lou, I've told Mr. Pickens over and over I don't want him to get the city attorney to sue J. Donald Jones for throwing us out on the street. I told him I wasn't giving any deposition. See, it was professional—that's why Mr. Pickens come over to my office this morning. It didn't have anything personal about it, I swear. He was just afraid if you saw me in there you'd think we were fooling around or something, which we weren't. I was just fixing his Ralph Lauren. It was knotted all wrong, his new tie."

"But how can that man—a deposition?"

". . . and Mr. Van Buren has done cut off my food stamps now," Mrs. Van Buren went on, grabbing another tissue from the box.

Lou has heard from Maigrite how unbalanced Mr. Van Buren became after winning $30 million in the lottery. Eighty-one years old, he sued the other two winners for slander and was awarded $3,000. Then he spent a week in jail for refusing to pay taxes on the $3,000. Finally, when a day trader lost $62,000 of his in a single hour, Mr. Van Buren stopped paying WaistWatch for the Total-PackageMakeover Mrs. Van Buren had gotten in lieu of a honeymoon. Because of Napoleonic law, he's even managed to swallow up all of Mrs. Van Buren's paychecks from Freds. That's why she never could pay Lou the rent after she ran away from Mr. Van Buren's mansion, which was exactly like Graceland, inside and out, only bigger. The reason Mrs. Van Buren had fled, Maigrite explained, was because her husband started rolling over her bare toes—on purpose. With the golf cart he used everywhere, even inside the house.

". . . and I'm going plum crazy living at my Mama's, Lou. I'm fixing to be fifty-six and still living at home. That can't be right. Mr. Pickens says I should just up and divorce Mr. Van Buren. I don't know why he tells me that since he knows I don't believe in divorce. Once you're married, that's it, brother. The end. He had his chance, you know, Mr. Pickens did. We used to date back in the Eighties, sort of . . ."

The mauve light starts flashing again. Lou presses the color-control monitor and in walks Mrs. Melvin Tudie. She, too, blinks to adjust to the dim flesh tones. But her stride is purposeful as she doesn't make a beeline toward the reception desk. True beelines, Lou has often been reminded by her husband, consist of abrupt zigzags, little dances. She has been asked not to use that term unless she's describing a drunk's progress. And Mrs. Tudie is decidedly not drunk.

"Brother Moodie, please," Mrs. Tudie says.

"Just a moment." As Lou depresses an incorrect extension, she can't help noticing the difference between the two women. Standing beside Mrs. Van Buren, Mrs. Tudie looks her age. At best, her liposuction has vacuumed off only five or ten minutes. In contrast, Mrs. Van Buren seems a good ten or fifteen years younger than the tax assessor—even though they're around the same age. Her skin, Mrs. Van Buren's, positively glows. The full-figure curves seem as voluptuous as a Renoir's. And her hair, though dyed and streaked with blond highlights, has the silky sheen of a teenager's. When WaistWatch gets ahold of you, Lou has to admit, they do a great job. It's yet another reason why she doesn't quit: Management really knows its business. And Lou is raking in three times as much as she ever did teaching theory and music appreciation at St. Jude Community College.

"I'm sorry. Brother Moodie doesn't seem to be in."

"That so? Why don't we try again, hon?"

Mrs. Tudie fingers the strap of her shoulder holster. Still in charge of the security agency while serving as tax assessor, the woman is licensed to carry a derringer.

"Is that alligator?" Mrs. Van Buren asks Mrs. Tudie as Lou dials for the correct temperature and time.

"Lizard. Holster is lizard."

"And this here's mother-of-pearl, right?" Mrs. Van Buren says, extracting the derringer from the holster.

"Correct," Mrs. Tudie says. Mrs. Van Buren gives the mother-of-pearl grip a fitful twirl or two.

Lou can see the headlines: RECEPTIONIST SLAIN IN TRAGIC MISHAP. For some reason, the thought is comforting. Think of the mileage Handgun Control could get out of it. Finally, she would have done something worthwhile with her life.

Mrs. Tudie plucks the derringer from Mrs. Van Buren's trigger finger. "This isn't a toy, Miss. We don't play with it. You want to buy yourself one, there's a sale over at City Hall this P.M. Confiscated firearms. Twenty-five bucks will get you peace of mind. Which reminds me—that computer you got, Mrs. Jones, the one in your guesthouse . . ."

"You mean my toolshed. And it's not a computer. It's just a printer."

"I heard you were illiterate. Computer illiterate."

"I don't know how to use computers, that's correct."

"Well, if it's just setting there, why not donate it to our sale?"

"Your gun sale?"

"We're selling a little bit of this and that. Flea market for my husband's campaign, state rep. He's running against that awful bitch who wants to outlaw assault weapons. Everyone's chipping in one way or another. Manning a booth or donating."

"Not everyone," Mrs. Van Buren puts in. "I'm voting for Georgina Mills."

"She's a socialist, you know. That what you want, Miss, a Communist running this district?"

"You bet your sweet ass, I do. Mama wanted me to rent *The Ten Commandments* the other night, and I said, 'Mama, I don't want you getting Moses mixed up in your head with Charlton Heston. Mr. Pickens told me that man's a kook, one of those subversives that don't believe in government.' That what *you* want, Miss? Some white militia nut running this district?"

Mrs. Tudie aims a look at Mrs. Van Buren that somehow ricochets to Lou, who mutters something about how sorry she feels for Mr. Heston.

"You'll be hearing from us, Mrs. Jones," the tax assessor says before turning smartly on her heels and marching out.

CHAPTER SIX

"**B**lue what?"

"Paint. I have to pick up some blue paint," Lou says to Mrs. Ompala as they cross the state line into Mississippi. Mrs. Ompala is in need of linens, and Lou has volunteered to help her find some at the mall in Eutaw. While she's at it, she will buy the paint needed to turn Maigrite's space back into a handicapped zone. Earlier that afternoon, the superintendent cited WaistWatch with a violation of USJ91.OSHA—by fax. Unless the matter was corrected within ten days, Brother Moodie would be paying a hefty fine.

"All this here," Lou says, gesturing expansively toward the pines bordering the highway, "this is not part of the Louisiana Purchase."

"Indeed," comes the voice from the back seat of the BMW. Mrs. Ompala couldn't ride in the front, Don explained to Lou before she drove away. She gets carsick seeing the lines come at her.

"The Louisiana Purchase itself is actually an illegal contract," Lou says with her eye on the rearview mirror. "Napoleon had no right to sell it to the United States without first offering Spain a chance to buy it back from France. Those were the terms of the sale from Spain to France in the first place. Quite frankly, I don't understand why Spain has let us get away with this all these years."

"Quite."

"Legally, most of the United States should be Spanish," Lou goes on, craning her neck around so Mrs. Ompala can hear better. The woman has a distracted look as she sips demurely from the bishop's silver flask. It's loaded with Don's ninety-year-old single malt, a guaranteed cure for carsickness, he assured her.

"The real illegal aliens—Mrs. Ompala, please don't open the door, that's the door handle. The real illegal aliens aren't the Mexicans crossing the border. They're—no, that lowers the window, Mrs. Ompala. You don't want the wind messing up your hat." The velvet cloche, held firmly in place by a diamond stickpin, looks oddly chic, like something a brash young performance artist with an NEA grant might sport. Lou herself could never get away with it, such a hat. She'd look old as the hills.

One more time Lou must warn Mrs. Ompala about the door handle, which makes her miss the turnoff for the mall. Ten minutes wasted now, since Lou will have to backtrack through downtown Eutaw.

Lou doesn't believe in malls. Whenever she can, she makes a point of not shopping in one. Mrs. Ompala listens to these sentiments with a thoughtful expression. They have paused by a fountain on their way to McCrae's, the store Lou imagines will have the best linens for Mrs. Ompala.

"I suppose you don't have malls in Mombasa, do you?" Lou asks. Dyed a severely antiseptic blue, water cascades into a basin of pennies. "I'd give my eyeteeth to live like that."

"Like what?"

Lou didn't mean to suggest that Mombasa is too primitive for malls. She's trying to say just the opposite, that Mrs. Ompala makes Eutaw seem Third World. Lou can't get over the weave of her companion's silklike suit. Never has she seen such material, a subtle mesh of pearl and the very faintest rose reflecting the luminous glow of her skin. Yet how can this be, a woman her age with skin so diaphanous? And the way the cloche sets off her hair, which is neither gray nor ash blond, neither silver nor pearl, but some combination that even allows for a hint of a rich, full-bodied chestnut. Lou marvels that other shoppers don't stop and stare. Do they not have eyes?

When they get to the household department of McCrae's, Lou tries to say something nice about Mombasa. She wants to reassure Mrs. Ompala, who seems as out of place here among the displays of percale and shams, as dazed and lost as an Anastasia.

"Why are we here?" Mrs. Ompala asks with the imperiousness of someone on the verge of collapse.

A weary clerk paws through sheets emblazoned with hunchbacks as Lou says, "Remember? You want to buy some linens."

"Linens, yes." She frees her gloved hand from Lou's tender grasp. "Not bedclothes."

Without Don to translate, Lou is momentarily at a loss. But then, gazing absently at a Disney label threatening full prosecution if something or other is violated, Lou gets it. *Linens* must mean *undergarments* in polite Mombasan society. The poor dear is trying to buy fresh panties. She's embarrassed to have Don launder anything at home.

"See, in America—I mean, I thought you didn't like the sheets at Don's—too slippery maybe, that satin. I slid out of bed once, landed right on my . . . Well, anyway, in Mombasa, you must have such wonderful fabrics, authentic hand-loomed . . ."

"Woman, what is all this nonsense about Mombasa? Why do you keep talking to me about Mombasa?"

"Isn't that Kenya, where you sailed from?"

"Twenty-five years ago, yes. I haven't laid eyes on it since."

Stung by the "woman," Lou trails behind Mrs. Ompala to the lingerie department. There she tries to be helpful, pointing out various bargains until Mrs. Ompala cuts her short. She can't think, she says, with someone hovering right next to her. Could she please have a few moments alone to make her selection?

On a bench by the fountain, Lou rehearses a discussion she will have with Don when she returns Mrs. Ompala to Coffee Ridge. What did he mean by telling her that the woman sailed from Mombasa? Is he intent on making a fool of her? Why, the way Mrs. Ompala looked at me, you'd think I was that Van Buren woman. That's exactly what I felt like, Don. Some scatterbrained ninny . . .

But that ninny, Lou reminds herself, was the one who spoke up against Charlton Heston while Lou just sat there, afraid her property tax might be raised. Lou simply can't help admiring Burma's courage, even though she shouldn't be getting herself mixed up with Maigrite's husband and . . .

Mrs. Ompala looms, but with no packages.

"Couldn't you find anything?"

"I'm afraid not, Dr. Jones. Come along. We'll try Saks."

"Saks? Why not Bergdorf's, the one next to Shoe Locker?" Normally, Lou is never catty. But Mrs. Ompala has hurt her feelings. She's . . . "Wait!"

"There's no Bergdorf's here," Lou says when she catches up with her charge. Amazing how efficiently Mrs. Ompala has propelled herself past Camelot, Mrs. Field's, and Chess King. With no effort at all, it seems, streamlined as a shark. Lou herself needs a moment to stop puffing. "No Saks, either. I was . . . just joking."

"Your husband assured me the mall has one."

"What? Oh, New Orleans, he meant. Lakeside Mall."

"Well?"

Could the woman really think she is anywhere near New Orleans? Did she not know north from south, the most primitive geography? "That's in the other direction. This is Mississippi, the state of Mississippi. New Orleans is much farther south, on the Mississippi River."

"I would have thought that by now, Dr. Jones, you would have learned the difference between a river and a state."

"But I—I mean Don didn't tell me you meant *that* mall. I just assumed . . ."

With pity tempering the exasperation in her pale blue eyes, Mrs. Ompala takes Lou by the elbow and steers her to a table in the Food Court. "A nice cup of tea, child. That will help you get a grip. We need to get ahold of ourselves, don't we?"

CHAPTER SEVEN

The China Wall has no hot tea. But Lou is able to get two cups of hot water for the price of coffee. She has come prepared with her own tea bags—Don's, actually.

"Of course, Don's mother nearly died when he married a Jew. Maybelle wouldn't even let him date me when we were in high school. We had to sneak around, pretend to be dating other people since she was such a strict Baptist."

Lou pours another drop from the bishop's flask into her tea.

"The bishop had several dear friends who were perverts," Mrs. Ompala says after accepting a drop in her own tea.

Lou, more puzzled than insulted, tries to insert something about how she has always adored men. But she is cut off by the older woman, who explains that *pervert* has nothing to do with sex. "We mean, of course, an Anglican who turns to Rome."

"I know," Lou says childishly. "I still don't see what this has to do with me."

"You did renounce your faith. For your mother-in-law."

Lou reaches for the bishop's flask. "For Maybelle? You got to be kidding. She thinks Episcopalians are worse than Jews. Almost as bad as R.C.'s. That was another reason I couldn't date Don. My dad was Catholic."

A child at a neighboring table screams fiercely for a gummi bear.

Mrs. Ompala's eyes, limpid as the waters of a brisk creek, seem to dance with secret musings.

"One time, Lord help us, Maybelle nearly caught me in her kitchen. Don was baking a German chocolate cake for me, my absolute favorite, and she came home early and . . ."

Lou pours another drop from the bishop's flask before going on: "It was like Romeo and Juliet, that's how we felt. Alpha knew, of course. She was the one who'd tell us when Maybelle was at the Jitney Jungle or the DAR. If it weren't for Alpha, Don and I never would've made it. That time he was baking the cake for me, it was Alpha who kept Maybelle talking in the living room so I could make my escape. I used to beg my mother to hire Alpha. It would have been so great to see Maybelle lose her precious maid—but, you know, in those days we could hardly afford the luxury of a maid and . . . Well, you know."

For a moment or two, Lou forgot the connection between this lady in silk opposite her and Alpha. "Of course," she amends, remembering, "that's what *Maybelle* called her. I hate that word myself. Even something like 'domestic engineer' is . . . I just don't think it's right for anyone to have someone like that in the house— I mean, working for you. Don's told you, I'm sure, how I wish Alpha would get a real job."

"That's quite enough, Jones."

"Not that housekeeping isn't real work, you know, with a certain dignity of its own. I didn't mean to imply that. It's just that Alpha is so intelligent, has so much potential. It makes my heart ache to think of a woman like her slaving away for Maybelle—I mean Maybelle's house was immaculate. Not a spot of dust anywhere. All those figurines, Alpha would dust each and every cow every single day. Can you believe someone would have cows in her house like that? And a cow cozy over the toilet paper? Maybelle even kept her NyQuil in a cow. Anyway, Alpha never complained. She'd serve mayonnaise in a cow, which was so hard to clean afterward. It's no wonder Maybelle adored Alpha. Of course, what

Alpha got out of it I'll never know. Peanuts, that's what she was paid. If I were her, I would have smashed every last cow in that woman's . . ."

"I said *enough*."

The pained look on Mrs. Ompala's face seems to age the woman, make her more plausibly the mother of a fifty-year-old domestic. Lou wants to reach out and take her hand, to restore her amazing ageless calm. And just as badly, she wants to know her story, how Mrs. Ompala had had the courage to marry an African, a black man. Considering how many years ago this was, back in the 1940s, this makes her a heroine in Lou's eyes. But then, how could Mrs. Ompala so easily let her sixteen-year-old daughter leave Kenya? And never see her for so many years afterward?

The lines etched now on Mrs. Ompala's face make Lou wary. She must be more careful. Such a delicate fabric, this tale of hers—so easily rent.

Nearby a teenager munching on a corn dog starts doling out Tater Tots to her children, three in all. Made a little self-conscious by them, Lou tries to think of something to break the uncomfortable silence at her table. "How terrible," Lou murmurs, "a girl her age, a mere child, having children herself. There should be a law. Nothing good can come of this. What possible future can this mother be giving her offspring . . ."

"How old are your offspring, Jones?"

Lou blushes. *Offspring*—such a silly word. Whatever made her say it? "Oh, Don and I don't believe it's right to overpopulate the earth. We decided long ago to help compensate for everyone who's straining the earth's resources."

"I see."

The mall's stale, recycled air, the tepid tea in a flimsy cup, the cramped seat, all make Lou feel the weariness of a transatlantic passenger on a chartered flight. Yet at the same time she's dogged by a tourist's faith that she's going somewhere important, that over these dark, fathomless time zones lie celebrated, ageless ruins. The real thing. No chintzy Vegas pyramids or antiseptic canals.

"And of course, Don—his sperm count, you know . . ."

Lou has never told a soul. Not even Maybelle knows the truth. Maybelle blames Lou, of course. She's always thought Lou is lacking something as a woman, isn't truly feminine.

"I didn't really mean to say that, Mrs. Ompala. Please, you won't tell anyone. I believe the bishop's tea has like . . . loosened my tongue. Not that Don would mind, really—he admires you so much—but . . . A drop more?"

Holding up a slender hand, gloved in ivory silk, Mrs. Ompala refuses the flask. "Of course, you've always wanted a child, haven't you?"

"No, no, I really do believe in overpopulation, how bad it is . . ." Lou twists her diamond ring, worth a year's salary at Waist-Watch, maybe more. "And besides, I've always been too busy for children. Right from the word go, I've never had a moment to spare. When I was at Florida State getting my doctorate"—and an abortion, from that one night with Melvin Tudie, right after she was elected Sweetheart of Delta Kappa Chi and Melvin was on trial for armed robbery, holding up an A&W for a root beer float as part of pledge week—"I worked for this horrible professor in Poultry Science who made me wake up two hundred and eighteen Rock Cornish hens at four-thirty every morning and take their temperature."

"I see."

Mrs. Ompala's steely eyes seem more gray than blue now. Lou freshens her tea with a drop from the bishop's flask. "In a way I'm almost glad that we can't have a child. I'm sure I'd have made a terrible mother. There's never been enough time. When I was teaching at St. Jude, I'd get home at eight or nine at night and have to leave at seven in the morning."

"Indeed."

"So, like . . . about Don, you won't say anything to him? What I said about him . . ." Lou swallows, as if trying to dislodge a lump of panic. "It doesn't matter to me, you know, not one iota. But Don, he's so sensitive. He'd think I really cared, as if he had failed me. So you see, you must promise me, Mrs. Ompala, you won't say a word to him."

"That's quite enough."

Lou wrings her large chapped hands, red from replacing a corroded joist under the sink at Coffee Ridge. "I just wanted to make sure you understood that . . ."

"You must stop sounding like a flibbertigibbet."

A curious mixture of shame and delight courses through Lou. The rebuke is so refreshing. Though the words are harsh, they're mitigated by a sweetly cadenced voice that almost sings. This faint music from afar, another age, tugs at a remote outpost of Lou's heart that has long ago been deadened by despair. And as numbed flesh revives, it stings.

"Well, I'm sorry if I . . . I was only trying to . . ." Lou pauses twice, waiting for Mrs. Ompala to insert an apology. "I suppose Tula Springs must seem filled with flibbertigibbets. I suppose after hobnobbing with Lady This and Lady That in . . . Just where did you say you came from?"

"I didn't."

"Oh." Primed to apologize in a catty way for being impertinent and not knowing her place, Lou remembers yet again that the woman has an African-American daughter. Who works as her maid.

"If you must know, Jones, I've been living in Houston."

"Oh, they have a superb opera company. Don drove me there to see *Moses und Aron*. Schoenberg. I brought the score with me. It's brutal, so difficult. I nearly cried for the poor singers, what they must endure."

Mrs. Ompala regards her cooly. "Mississippi. Houston, Mississippi. My husband has a few acres there . . ."

"*Shoppers, attention,*" a loudspeaker blares as Mrs. Ompala says something about harvesting pecans.

"*A special two-for-one sale on all specially marked items is now in progress at Camelot Music . . .*"

The lilt in Mrs. Ompala's voice Lou strains to interpret as she would an unfamiliar Schubert lied. But now a shriek makes it even harder to know what the woman is saying. The smallest child at the next table—no more than two years old, maybe three—is pounding the *Tommy Hilfiger* emblazoned on his mother's sweat-shirt.

"I'm sorry, Mrs. Ompala. I didn't quite catch . . . Did you say something about pecans?"

"We would harvest them. For confections."

"In Houston?"

"Houston's the nearest town. We were in the country."

"Where is Houston? The Delta?"

"No. The other side of the state. Near Tupelo."

But this is impossible. Such style, such elegance, cannot possibly have come from Elvis country.

"Surely you weren't born there, Mrs. Ompala. You're not really . . ."

"I was born in Mombasa."

"Do they have bishops there? Is that where your uncle, the bishop . . ."

"The bishop's palace is near Evesham. Originally, Eoveshomme, named after a ninth-century swineherd, Eoves. Apparently, one of Eoves's pigs went astray and as he was out searching for it . . ."

Oh, please shut the heck up! Lou glares at the neighboring table. She can't hear what Mrs. Ompala is saying now, something about a virgin. With an even fiercer shriek, the pale child wrenches the container from his mother's creamy-white hand and hurls the Tater Tots into the dank air.

Gracefully as a teenager, Mrs. Ompala leans over and plucks one of the reconstituted potatoes from the floor. When she pops it into her mouth, the child gapes, his watery-blue eyes wide.

"She gonna get herself good and sick," the weary teen mutters as she wheels the boy and his twin sisters away. The overloaded double stroller bumps into a nonfunctional pillar before steering clear of the Food Court.

Mrs. Ompala's chair scrapes the plastic tiling. "There's a shirt-waist you must see, Jones. Come along."

Lou just sits there. Beneath her veil, Mrs. Ompala raises an eyebrow. How odd that Lou hasn't noticed the veil before, so delicately woven that she can't quite tell where it ends. Or has she just lowered the veil from her cloche?

"I'm sorry, you were saying something about a virgin? In Africa?"

"*The* Virgin. Evesham Abbey is built on the spot where she appeared to Eoves, the swineherd. That's how we were fed after my father contracted dengue fever. My mother sold souvenirs at the Abbey shop. Evesham, of course, is in Worcestershire, my dear, not Africa. She died of homesickness, Mother did. She longed for Africa cruelly. Her exile in Evesham was quite bitter, selling trinkets to tourists. Mostly a trickle of Anglo-Catholics. Some R.C.'s. Now come along, please. You must see this shirtwaist."

"Do you really think you should have eaten that potato?" Lou asks. "Why did you . . ."

"It will look splendid on you, Jones. Come along. And mind the bishop."

Lou's alligator purse nearly knocked over the silver flask. As she hands it back to Mrs. Ompala, she notices for the first time the peach so delicately limned in the crown sterling. Without a certain slant of light, it's invisible.

CHAPTER EIGHT

The Morgen house sits squarely in what would have once been called the wrong side of the tracks in Tula Springs. Hollywood, as the neighborhood is known, consists largely of neglected shotgun cabins that some citizens might go a few blocks out of their way to avoid, especially at night, as they head for Wal-Mart. A screened-in porch, the gallery, wraps the entire wood-frame structure, which from the front seems to be a single story, but actually contains three separate floors. As deep as it is wide, the home has twice the area of the lavish houses in Lou's gated community. But because it is obscured by a grove of massive live oaks, one just an acorn when Anne Boleyn was wed, the overall effect is of quiet restraint. It's only after you've rocked gently down the oystershell drive that the proportions are corrected. Lou often feels dwarfed as she climbs the concrete stairs to the gallery. Indeed, each step seems a few inches higher than contractors would allow today, as if people back in 1880, when the house was built, could all slam dunk with ease.

As an old friend, someone who has known Grady Morgen since nursery school, Lou never has to knock. A key under the rush doormat lets her in, and then it's simply a matter of pressing the code on the alarm system—Grady's father's birthday. It's easy to remember—1913—since it's the same year as Lou's father's. A refugee from Bavaria, Lou's father had lived for a while on the Morgen property in a toolshed visible only from a certain angle in the third-floor library, the shed nestled in the ground-hugging limbs of the Boleyn oak. In 1933, Hartmund Vogelsanger had been studying to be a priest when the Nazis, just before the Concordat with the Vatican, shut down the seminary. Herr Vogelsanger had been foolish enough to voice doubts about the regime's euthanasia and racial policies to his bishop, who reported him to the authorities. He was arrested, but after serving six months of hard labor, managed to flee on foot to Switzerland.

Before winding up in Tula Springs, Lou's father had eluded the INS by stealthy moves from Bay Ridge to Camden, from Milwaukee to New Orleans. Judge Morgen, delighted to find someone as passionate about Latin as he was, turned out to be more of a friend than a landlord. He and Herr Vogelsanger would spend entire evenings discussing Ovid and Livy in the toolshed, much to the disgust of Grady's mother. When the KKK tried to burn a cross outside the toolshed—Catholics were not appreciated during the Depression—Judge Morgen strolled out with his shotgun and blasted the ringleader, who, once the hood was removed, turned out to be his own brother-in-law. Judge Morgen was convicted of attempted murder, but his sentence was suspended by the presiding judge, who owed his election to a $35 contribution from Judge Morgen.

Lou has always harbored a special admiration for Judge and Mrs. Morgen, who hadn't let the trial destroy their marriage. Mrs. Morgen had actually testified against her husband, recalling how he had always had it in for her brother, always looking for some excuse to do him in. Of course, that was in the days when divorce was unheard of. You stuck together no matter what. Mrs. Morgen hadn't exactly encouraged the friendship between Grady and Lou. In fact, she would leave the room whenever Lou was brought over by Judge Morgen's chauffeur to play. Lou, ignorant then of the history she was burdened with, simply thought Mrs. Morgen was peculiar, strangely shy for a grown-up.

Lou's parents had never even mentioned the trial. It was her mother-in-law who had filled Lou in while trying to persuade Lou not to become an Episcopalian, that the Baptists were the only hope for her immortal soul. Judge Morgen belonged in jail, Maybelle said, and yet there he was, bold as brass, teaching Sunday School at Frederik Memorial. Of course, it was Maybelle's calling Judge Morgen a corrupt, bloodstained godless traitor to all the South held dear that had helped Lou decide to become an Episcopalian.

Vast enough to accommodate one of Hollywood's shotgun shacks, the Morgen kitchen seems as archaic as a nunnery's in a thriving Calvinist port. A pocked and pitted sink, not half as deep as Lou's stainless steel, always splashes when you rinse. The cast-iron oven, once fueled by wood, can cook no turkey larger than nine pounds, a fact Lou had discovered one Thanksgiving when she tried to squeeze in the tom her husband had shot off a telephone wire in front of Western Auto. Even the counter space is stingy. Lou must chop onions on a stool because Frederik, Grady's daughter, has cluttered the one decent counter with her Hittite shards. A recent Yale graduate, Fred is spending a few days with her mother before going on a dig in Israel with her father, a Vassar professor who divorced Grady shortly after Frederik was born. Grady has since dropped her married name—and when Judge and Mrs. Morgen died, moved into the house she inherited, here, alone.

"Three days doesn't seem much," Lou says as she wipes away a tear. "Considering that she and Alex will be together six weeks in Israel."

"Stay out of it, Lou. I don't want you going upstairs and talking to her."

Stung by the injustice of the remark, Lou minces a Vidalia too finely. As if she were a busybody, butting in where she doesn't belong. She is, after all, the girl's godmother.

"Enough with the onions, Lou. Check on the eggs."

Egg salad sandwiches they're making, three dozen for a reception to honor a St. Jude Community College alumna, Cheryl Ames, who's been invited to sing at Bayreuth. Caviar and lox will be provided by WaistWatch, thanks to Lou, who persuaded Brother Moodie

a few months ago that a substantial donation to the Tula Springs
Arts Council would be good publicity.

"I'm hoping Mrs. Ompala will come," Lou says as she starts on
another onion. Grady, with her Ole Miss degree, can sometimes
play high and mighty. From time to time one must remind her that
not everyone on earth is her handmaid. "I have a feeling, though,
that she might try to back out. She doesn't seem to like Wagner. I
shouldn't have told her the Ames girl is singing the love-death
thing."

Glancing over at Grady, Lou waits for her to say something reassuring. But Grady is preoccupied with the eggs, tapping the
shells with a spoon. Once a beauty, a star of sorts at Ole Miss,
Grady now affects to be plain. She does nothing with her hair, her
bangs resembling those of the Dutch Cleanser girl, and she wears
khaki trousers and a sweatshirt to the WinnDixie. Even at the Co-
mus ball in New Orleans last year, she refused any adornment but
pearls, not even a touch of lipstick. And the Valentino she wore
was thirty years old. Yes, she's still fit enough to wear what she
bought when she was married. Grady walks six miles a day around
Hollywood with her mutts from the pound, Alice and Horace.

"I was thinking we might grab a bite before the recital, Grady.
Maybe ask Mrs. Ompala to join us. You'd like to meet her, wouldn't
you?"

"No."

"I'll pick you up at five-thirty. We'll take her to that restaurant
on North Gladiola that looks like it's going out of business. I feel
so sorry for it. No one's ever there. And they try so hard. Arugula in
their salad, radicchio. And I swear they had truffles once, black
truffles."

"Lou, I'm not paying thirty bucks for a plate of spaghetti."

"We'll have fun. Mrs. Ompala is absolutely the most fascinat-
ing woman you'll ever meet. I'm so afraid she's going to get tired of
us and move back to Mississippi. We've got to show her how . . ."

"Oh, God—dinner with Blanche Dubois, just what I've always
wanted."

"Don't be silly. She's really from Africa, you know—Mombasa. That's where she was born." Lou is about to add something about the bishop, Mrs. Ompala's uncle, and Lady Fitzhoward, but censors herself in time. Grady hates any sort of pretension.

"We'll have fun, Grady. I'll pick you up at five-thirty."

Grady whisks the knife away from Lou. "Enough with the onions, girl. We got all those eggs to chop."

From the sink, Lou steps up her attack on Grady's complacency. Just maybe there was something new under the sun, something worth her making a little effort to find out about. Peeling away the hot shells, Lou goes on and on about Mrs. Ompala, how the woman must have such a story. Imagine, back in the Forties or Fifties, what courage it had taken to fall in love with a black man— and then marry him, have his child. Why it positively killed her father, must have. She says it was some kind of fever did him in, but that didn't fool me. Is it any wonder her mother had left Africa, gone back to England? Then, as if all that wasn't enough, Mrs. Ompala had stuck by her husband when he decided to leave Mombasa. Going with him to Mississippi, of all places. The only white woman in a black household. And in a virtual police state.

"Lou, look at the mess you're making." Grady scoops a handful of shells from the drain. "God."

"I'll pay for your dinner, Grady—if that's what you're worried about."

"It's not the dough. Life is too short, Bear. I've spent my whole life pleasing horrible bores. No more. Finito. I'm fifty-three and I'm going to damn well do what I please."

"I guarantee you won't be bored. Cross my heart. By the way, do you like my shirtwaist? Mrs. Ompala picked it out. Says it's me."

Grady plucks an eggshell from the chenille-like fabric of Lou's recent purchase. "Why do you make such a big deal out of someone from Mississippi?"

"Think, Grady—how brave it was for her to love then. Mrs. Ompala could have been thrown in jail for miscegen— Oh, Alice!"

One of the mutts has scrambled up onto the counter and

buried its snout in the mayonnaise. Grady gathers the lank beast into her arms and plants a kiss on its damp nose. "Don't mind her, Horace. She didn't mean to call you a girl."

"What's wrong with being called a girl? Anyway, Grady, you got to make more of an effort with people. Especially someone new."

"I've made plenty of effort."

"Yeah, like when?"

"How many times did I have that Mondrian girl over here."

"Maigrite. The answer is once. Just once. You barely gave her a chance."

Grady's laugh is more like a cough. "I ought to report you to the Better Business Bureau. False advertising. The way you went on about her. 'Maigrite is so lovely, positively the most beautiful woman you've ever seen, all because of her suffering, the fever. Gave her such a haunted look. Grew up so poor she couldn't even get fitted with a proper leg brace. Eight brothers and sisters, never got enough to eat. Thin as a rail.' That's right, Lou, you had me expecting some Madonna in a wheelchair. And then in struts this little hussy, Miss Priss."

Grady's cook had made vichyssoise for that dinner—and when Bill, the butler, served it, Maigrite asked him to take it back, complaining that it was too warm, not properly chilled.

"It was her husband's fault, Mr. Pickens'. I didn't realize he was coming, too. He has a genius for bringing out the worst in Maigrite."

Grady tosses to Horace, back on the floor now, a slice of her cook's homemade rye. The cook is from the Bronx, Co-op City. "And then your boss. I made an effort with him."

"Well, you *did* sign up for his aerobics."

"The only way I could get him out of the house. I swear, Lou, I really think if Bill hadn't been hanging around that night, your darling Brother Moodie might have ravished me."

Don't flatter yourself, Lou wants to reply. "You have to admit," she says instead, "he's done wonders with you. You really do look great, your waist."

Frowning, Grady orders Lou to put the eggshells in Bill's compost bag so they'll fertilize the lawn. Then she squeezes a tick off Alice, who's trotted into the kitchen with a Barbie dangling from her jaws. "That man's got a screw loose, rapping for Jesus. I can't stand whitebread who think they can rap."

"But it works, Grady. You got to admit. What are you, one-fifteen now?"

"You're crazy to stay there. I'll never figure out how a friend of mine ended up going Jesus freak on me."

"I'm not a Jesus freak."

"And thrusting your Jesus freak friends on me. Is this Impala woman a freak, too?"

"Just the opposite. Mrs. Ompala is very High Church. Even-song and all that."

"From bad to worse," Grady mutters to Alice, who's in her arms now, lolling blissfully.

"For someone who practically runs the entire church, bossing the poor pastor around, giving the curate a reading list, you sound . . ."

"Let's not get into that. No, Alice, not that again." She buries her face in the mutt's rubbery belly.

"Did it ever occur to you, Grady, that some people might be Christian and yet underneath it all be decent and good-hearted? Now look." With a pair of tongs, Lou plucks Alice's Barbie out of the pot of boiling new potatoes. "I hope you're satisfied." She lets the doll drop to the floor, next to the built-in drain. "The potatoes are ruined. We'll have to start all over again."

"Don't be silly. There's nothing wrong with that doll. Where you off to, girl?"

"The ladies'."

"You're going to talk to Fred, aren't you? Leave the girl alone. If my own daughter thinks I'm only worth three days of her precious time, two and a half, actually, then . . ."

Lou doesn't deign to reply. Grady knows she has a bladder problem. That's all she's doing.

After a brief Number One upstairs, Lou comes to a practical conclusion: She might as well be hanged for a sheep as a lamb. Under the pretext of wanting to know why the Linnaean system is out of fashion at Yale these days, Lou raps verbally on Fred's open door. Carolus Linnaeus, Fred explains, distorted reality with un-Darwinian, white male classifications that don't reflect a fluid . . . Lou nods, appending a footnote about how hurt Grady is. Hurt? Fred looks mystified, then asks if she can borrow Lou's Colt .45, the one Don gave her for Christmas last year. Lou asks why she wants it. Because, Fred says, if she hears another word about staying longer, she's going to shoot herself. Lou says she's sorry, but she tossed the gun away—into Tula Creek on Boxing Day.

Before Lou returns to the new potatoes downstairs, Fred has agreed to spend a full week with her mother on the way back from Tel Aviv.

CHAPTER NINE

"I forgot."

"You forgot?" Maigrite cascades a window. "You go all the way to the mall in Mississippi for a can of blue paint and forget to buy it?"

"It wasn't just to buy a can of paint. I had things of my own to attend to."

It's been a slow day at WaistWatch. This squabbling over the paint is vaguely refreshing, Lou finds, for it helps pass the time. Lou dials the weather—partly cloudy—and then Coffee Ridge. Alpha picks up and tells Lou that Don and Mrs. Ompala have gone to Lakeshore Mall in New Orleans. Lou asks if Alpha's had any luck finding an apartment for her mother. Does she think she really might stay in Tula Springs? Alpha switches off the vacuum and says, "What?" When Lou repeats herself Alpha says she doesn't have time to talk now. She has work to do.

It's always been this way with Alpha. When she comes to clean Lou's house, she'll never sit down for a cup of coffee, a pleasant chat. It would be so much fun to hash over those days when Alpha tricked Maybelle so that Lou could neck with Don, right in Maybelle's own house. And now there's so much Lou wants to know about Alpha and her mother. Just what did they say to each other after all those years of separation? Was Alpha angry at her mother, resentful? Or glad to see her? How does she feel about having a mother who's so . . . Caucasian? But Alpha just does her chores and leaves, cash in hand.

Maigrite turns up the volume on the television that entertains clients waiting for an appointment. Lou asks if she would mind turning it down a notch or two. It's an exercise tape, three women stretching together on a beach. One of them is Lynda, circa 1991, clad in a shimmering Lycra bodysuit that seems modest at first glance, less so with a steadier look. Her somewhat dated Afro is not affected by the Caribbean breeze. In this video, Lynda could almost be a younger, shapelier Angela Davis. Since then, Lynda's Afro has been reborn as a lustrous copper mane.

Maigrite aims her remote. Lynda continues singing her hymn of praise, unheard now. Palm fronds shiver in Nassau . . .

Around noon Maigrite informs Lou she can't have lunch with her today because she has to drive Burma over to Wal-Mart. Lou sighs.

"What?" Maigrite says as she appliqués a reindeer to the sleeve of a red-and-green sweater. Maigrite creates her own designs from arts-and-crafts kits she stashes in her desk. "What do you want?"

"Nothing."

"You look like you're about to say something."

How Maigrite can be so blind about her husband and Burma Van Buren, Lou finds hard to believe. "Burma told me your husband is thinking of suing us. He's been talking to her and . . ."

"The superintendent can't sue anyone. He's not a lawyer."

"I know, but he wants the city attorney to see if any civil rights were violated. Honestly, Maigrite, I don't think it's such a good idea, all the time he spends with Burma. Interviewing her, I mean. I think he's trying to stir up something."

Maigrite tilts the felt reindeer at a jauntier angle. "Burma's not going to sue you, girl. Relax. She's got a heart of gold, lets everyone walk all over her."

"Well . . . Anyway." The fumes from Maigrite's glue gun are making Lou lightheaded. "Is that a Christmas gift? It's nice."

For Lou's birthday last year, Maigrite gave her a taupe sweater, on which were glued pumpkins and ghosts. Lou forces herself to wear it to the office every now and then in October just so Maigrite's feelings won't be hurt.

"Christmas? Girl, you crazy? It's September."

"I know. I just thought you were getting a head start."

Maigrite aims and fires again at the reindeer. "I hate people who do that, start shopping so early for Christmas. The superintendent buys my presents every year on Lincoln's Birthday. Here, hold this reindeer still." She grabs Lou's index finger and sets it on an antler.

"Please be careful with that gun. Oh, Maigrite!"

"What?"

"You got glue all over my hand. It's hot!"

"I get glue on me all the time. Washes right off." She holds up the sweater for Lou to admire. "You think Alpha will like it?"

"My ring, too. It's on my diamond." Lou plucks a tissue from a box near Maigrite's scanner. "This better come off. I . . . Alpha? What are you giving her a sweater for?"

"She helped me out with this dinner party I gave for Brother Moodie."

Lou stops rubbing the diamond. "You wouldn't want her full-time, would you?"

"What? A full-time guest?" Maigrite eyes the reindeer critically.

"Alpha was a guest?"

"No, Lou, we just asked her over to scrub the floors."

"I'm serious, Maigrite. How do you know her? She's never mentioned . . ."

"Alpha and the superintendent are taking the same course at St. Jude. Macroeconomics."

"What? That's impossible."

"Good heavens, Louise. Don't tell me you didn't know she's going to night school."

"Of course, I knew. It's just—I didn't realize, your husband, they were, the same class and all. It seems so . . ."

"So what? Look, I got to run. Want me to bring you back some-thing for lunch?"

Lou mutters a *no*. Then tacks on a *thank you*.

Munching a lo-cal Cranbran muffin, Lou reads, *"The truth was, Witt loved them all, passionately, with an almost sexual ecstasy of comradeship. Even Bugger Stein and Welsh . . ."*

"Sister Lou?"

With a start, Lou glances up. Brother Moodie is beaming down upon her with a hearty smile. Handsome in an old-fashioned, Vic-torian way, Brother Moodie brings a blush to Lou's cheeks as she slips the novel into her handbag. She likes the man, the exuberant tawny waves on his leonine head, the massive torso padded with a sense of homely comfort. Something about him amuses her, makes her feel vaguely tickled, glad that this throwback to a robust, un-apologetic manhood is here on this planet, in this town, this rail-road station.

"We were sorry to miss Sister Lou at our fellowship," Brother Moodie says.

"What fellowship?"

"Sister Maigrite went all out. Crabmeat cocktails and duck à l'orange. Everyone got his own personal duck."

Lou smiles bravely. "I'm afraid I wasn't invited, Brother Moodie."

"Sure you were. Miss Ruth said your husband was under the weather."

"What? Don never said a word to me about . . . And who is this Ms. Ruth anyway?"

"I asked her to speak to Don about our new program. You'd get an employee discount, Sister Lou. Our plan is to inaugurate CIC on Washington's Birthday."

"Sick?"

"Couples In Crisis. By exorcising your mutual hatred with kick-boxing, you'll find that you and the mister . . ."

"Good heavens, Brother Moodie. Don and I haven't the slightest need to step into the ring. We've never gotten along better, and I think this Miss Buttinsky, whoever she is, has a lot of nerve to . . ."

"Calm down, Sister Lou. I'm sure your housekeeper has only your best interests at heart."

"Housekeeper? I don't have any Ruth working for me."

Her desk groans as he perches on the edge. Though his office is hung with glossies of his prize-winning physique—Mr. Las Vegas in 1979, Mr. ISBN in 1980, embracing George Bush in 1982—he's always modestly clad in baggy mauve workout suits for his discipling. "Surely you know that isn't her real name, Sister Lou. Ruth Amakenyatta despaired of anyone *here* being able to get it right. So she just uses the first letter. Greek, you know."

"Of course I know it's Greek." She shuffles some papers as newscasters do while reading from a monitor. "Now if you don't mind, Brother Moodie, I'm very busy."

"Why are you reading James Jones?"

Lou realizes he can't see through her Coach handbag, that he probably caught a glimpse before she stowed the novel away. Nevertheless, it's unsettling, the way he seems to see through everything. "My book club voted for it. I campaigned for Susan Sontag."

"Against Interpretation?"

Lou blushes, as if he's guessed a shameful secret. But how could he possibly know this? Her heart pounds from the curious intimacy, the polyester mauve lapping her Coach bag. Was there nothing hidden from him?

Set off by the ornate gold of a vulgar class ring, a diamond shimmers as he combs a finger through his lush, graying sideburns. "By the way, Sister Lou, what about that handicapped space? Miss Tudie is breathing fire down my neck."

Like a broken dike, Lou allows a torrent of explanation to spew forth. She never mentioned the violation to him because it's really all Lynda's fault for not making parking easier for Maigrite with her anorexia and you see how . . .

Brother Moodie smiles. "Let's just find us some blue paint, Sister Lou. Keep City Hall happy."

"I'm sorry if I . . . but I was just trying to help Maigrite and . . ."

"No need to feel sorry. You do a bang-up job here. And we love you. You know that, don't you? We all love you something awful."

So firm, so masculine, a hand envelops hers. And yet the grip is gentle as a woman's. No hint of liberties being taken, only a sense of reassurance that all is well.

If Grady Morgen happened to come back for the cross-training shoes she left behind, she would have caught a glimpse of Lou's boss gently stroking her chapped red hands. All Grady's suspicions about her aerobics instructor—that Brother Moodie was just a sleazy Vegas sex machine—would have been confirmed. If Lou had been able to summon up the courage to tell her best friend the truth, Grady wouldn't have believed it. But it's doubtful whether Lou could have told everything. How could she admit to someone as honest and blameless as Grady Morgen that she, Lou, had once broken down in Brother Moodie's office? Before Don had moved out of the house, Lou was in the grip of an endless postop depression. What was supposed to have been simple bunion surgery turned into a disaster after a nurse gave her pain medication that she was allergic to. The bunion itself never healed properly, and soon, against her will, Don was suing three doctors and a hospital supply company. Lou was especially embarrassed since two of these doctors' wives were on the Arts Council with her. Yes, Don was only asking for what was her due, simple justice, but Lou plummeted into a real depression with all the depositions and endless paperwork. She just couldn't bear for Don to touch her during this time. That was when she had asked Brother Moodie to help her, to take her in his arms, just hold her. He had come out from behind his desk and pulled her close in a tender embrace. But when she began to press her lips against the mauve, he took a step away. Gently, graciously, without actually saying it, he refused.

Grady Morgen did not burst in on them, though. The thought only haunts Lou after Brother Moodie has gone to lunch. As Lou retrieves *The Thin Red Line*—Grady's suggestion for book club— from her handbag, she wonders whether she could have explained to Grady the truth about that hand over hers. It wouldn't have been just a question of her own courage, but of protecting Don. If he ever found out what she'd done, Lou was certain, it would kill him, finish him off for good. And Lou herself is still not sure whether she was rejected for morality's sake, out of respect for the Ten Commandments emblazoned on the restroom door—or whether she simply isn't attractive enough to be unfaithful.

CHAPTER TEN

"Well, what did you think of her?"

Bill, the butler, is going to drive Mrs. Ompala home. Lou, who should have driven Mrs. Ompala back to Coffee Ridge, can't wait until morning for the verdict. She has to know Grady's opinion right away.

"She's O.K., I guess."

"O.K.? That's all you can say?"

"Help me with these dishes."

Dinner had been served on the east gallery. A ceiling fan churned the muggy October air, cooling the diners and the stuffed portobellos Lou had supplied. They went so well with the redfish Grady's cook netted herself in Lake Pontchartrain. As the butler's headlights sweep the drive, live-oak limbs look almost readable, like Arabic script, but disappear too soon to be deciphered. The lean frogs in these limbs would make a pleasant accompaniment to their chat if only Grady would stop fussing with the dirty dishes— and the good silverware Lou had insisted she use. You never knew about Grady. Once she served the governor, an old friend of her father's, Gallo in a jelly glass.

"For heaven's sake, Grady. Let Bill clean up."

"I can't do that."

"Why not? It's his job, isn't it?"

That Acura of his, turning now into the street, costs more than most houses in the neighborhood. Bill is an ex-boyfriend of Frederik, who placed him with her mother after Bill dropped out of Yale to write on spec for *Inside Edition*. It's Bill who insists on the title "butler," mainly to gall his father, that CFO of a *Fortune* 500 database firm. Bill writes in his own suite on the third floor, complete with bath, library, and separate entrance. When he turns twenty-three next year, he'll be able to dip into the trust fund set up by his grandparents. Until then, his father has cut him off without a cent. Not for being gay, the father has insisted over the phone more than once to Lou, who sometimes picks up the receiver when Grady is detained. It's for being a butler. No self-respecting son of his would ever think of taking such a job.

"I feel funny making a young man like Bill, so bright and earnest . . . Here, kid."

"Thanks," Lou says as the china is unloaded into her chapped hands. The screen door that she tries to yank open with a free pinky has swollen in its frame, won't budge. She kicks at it vainly, then returns her burden to the mahogany table. "You got to fix this stupid door, Grady. No, don't look at me. Get that boy genius to plane it himself. You still got my planer. Yes, you do. When I fixed the third-floor doors for you last week, I left it upstairs. Now what? Don't blow those out."

"They're beeswax."

"Aren't I good enough for beeswax?" Lou lights the extinguished wick with the flame of another taper. "Ouch! That darn wax."

"Are you just going to leave those dishes there? Help me tidy up."

Lou helps by finishing the Cakebread merlot in Grady's glass. It looks neater empty. "Bill could have served the salad. Why did *I* have to get up and   "

"He had an inspiration. Had to write it down. And it was me who got the salad. You only tossed it."

Silently, Grady offers Lou a toke on her weed, which Lou waves away. They've already argued about the grass Bill supplies

Grady with. Fewer calories than booze, Grady has explained to Lou. And besides, Brother Moodie forbids anyone in his aerobics class to drink.

"How about putting that thing like totally out? That's all I need, getting hauled in by Tudie's goons. Don't laugh."

Grady isn't. She's coughing. Smoke must have gone down the wrong pipe. Not quite as adept, apparently, as in the good ole days. Grady once told Lou that she never would've been able to endure a second at Ole Miss without her weed. Stoned out of her mind, Grady fit in perfectly with the other debs in her sorority, who thrived on a weird, homegrown sort of high.

"So come on, Grady—did you notice her skin, Mrs. O's, how perfect it is? It's really incredible."

"Anyone looks good in candlelight. Especially when you're half blind. Whatever did happen to my glasses, girl? I could've sworn they were right on that thing by you . . ."

"When I'm with her, I feel as if I've stepped back in time—into late James, where you're not quite sure what all the antecedents are, but it's too vulgar to ask."

Grady rummages around for her glasses, which Lou, now that Mrs. Ompala has left, discreetly returns to the Adam commode beside her.

"I've never met anyone with so much . . . class."

"There they are!" Grady pounces on the thick tortoiseshell frames that make her look like a hopeless spinster. They ride askew, a little cockeyed, with a bit of Scotch tape to reinforce a faulty hinge. "I just knew they were here. It happens to me all the time. I set something down and it just . . . like disappears."

"Yes, Grady, like far out. Anyway, this woman has class, real class. A certain breeding you don't see anymore these days."

"Back to the good old days when everyone knew his place. Sho nuff, massa."

"I'm serious. Look at my dad. He resoled shoes. But he translated Origen. And your own father, reading Marcus Aurelius every morning during breakfast, out loud."

"So delightful with grits."

"Your father knew what real quality was. He loved my dad."

"Daddy dearest was a racist pig."

The blades of the ceiling fan twirl as languidly as an Ealing Studios prop. *Rain,* perhaps, starring Leslie Howard. "He may have been racist, but he wasn't a pig. No one who loved my father could be a real pig."

Grady sucks the finger that got too close to the burning weed. She spares nothing. "You're crazy, you know. This dame you've taken up with, she said so herself. When you went to take a whiz . . . Are those fireflies? Could there be fireflies in February?"

"Try October, Grady. What did she say?"

"Something about you and Bill. October? I mean Don, you and Don."

Lou feels her hackles rise. "Go on."

"She thinks you've got the most something marriage she's ever seen. 'Seemly'—or was it 'suitable'? Well, whatever."

Whether feathers or fur—Lou's uncertain what they are—the hackles subside. Lou stuffs the cork back in the bottle. She no longer thirsts. "I thought she said I was nuts."

"Well, that, too. Only someone a little dotty could put up with a man like J. Donald Jones. That's what she said."

"*Me* dotty? I like that. When we were in the mall in Mississippi . . ."

"Made me laugh—you and Don, the perfect couple."

"What's so funny about that?"

"Well, like here you are, separated, on the verge of divorce, and she says she's never seen a better marriage."

"I told you, it's only temporary. Don's not really living in Coffee Ridge. He's just guarding his folks' property. That loony librarian could come back any day with a court order. Pickens wants the city attorney to sue us for housing discrimination."

"I really should do these dishes," Grady says, stacking plates in a haphazard way, still slouched in her chair.

"Pickens is friends with the woman I rented Coffee Ridge out to, Burma Van Buren. And Burma sublet it to some friends of hers who are lesbians, and Don . . ."

"Look, girl, the man isn't a lawyer."

"I know . . ."

"And our dear superintendent of garbage has problems of his own."

"What? You know him?"

"Alpha told me all about him. She goes to school with him, those night classes at St. Jude."

"What were you doing with Alpha?"

"Lunch. She asked me to lunch at that joint on North Gladiola and . . ."

Some forks Lou picked up clatter into the porringer.

"What's got into you?" Grady says as Lou marches into the kitchen, her arms loaded with far too many dishes.

"You want to clean up for your poor genius butler, right? Well, I'm cleaning."

"Why so pissed, Bear? For having lunch with your maid?"

"Don't be ridiculous. She's not my . . . When are you going to get a dishwasher? You're the worst skinflint I've ever known, Grady. Not that that stops you from having lunch at a place you told *me* you couldn't afford."

"It was a business lunch, girl."

"What possible business can you have with Alpha? Does she remember nothing about your father, how he . . ." Judge Morgen had blocked the voter registration drive that Lou's mother had initiated in the Sixties. Back then Lou's mother had conducted the band in the black high school, and now it's *Grady* who's invited to lunch. Lou can't even get Alpha to have a cup of coffee with her.

"Don't use so much water," Grady says, turning off the tap. "You know she's just been elected president of the Foreign Students Caucus at St. Jude."

"Alpha? You're not serious."

"They want to get rid of the provost."

"Rowena? What's wrong with Rowena?"

Grady flicks an ash into a Qianlong vase. "Looks like Row made herself a boo-boo. Hired that Whitney fellow as dean of resource management."

"But he's black. How can the Caucus object to that?"

"Alpha says it's sexist. Dr. Smith was much more qualified."

"Who's Dr. Smith?"

"You've met her, Bear. In May, the book club—she was our guest. Smart as a whip, that gal. Ph.D. from Stanford, teaches chemistry at St. Jude."

"May? That was *Buddenbrooks*. I thought it was a Filipina woman who talked about Mann."

"Right. Gloria Luz Smith. She's the one Alpha thinks should've been dean." As Grady leans over to turn off the hot water tap again, ashes flutter into the sink.

"I think Dr. Whitney was a good choice," Lou says, turning the water back on. "I hope you're planning to stick by Rowena."

"Alpha says he got his degree from a community college in Alabama."

"What's wrong with that? All this snobbery about schools is ridiculous. I've known people from Stanford and Yale who were complete idiots."

The greenish smoke from the grass is making Lou dizzy. Her heart pounds fiercely, out of kilter. All this news of Alpha—not only going to school, but president . . . And not a word to her, Lou.

Grady stubs out the joint in the porringer. "I'm beat. Night, Bear." She waves away a mosquito—or maybe it's a good-night wave. "Leave those dishes, girl. I'll be real mad if you like . . ." She heads up the back stairs, built for servants.

If it really would get Grady angry, Lou would summon the strength to do the dishes. But she knows enough to let them be.

After blowing out the candles on the gallery, Lou returns to the kitchen and collapses onto the horsehair sofa. A Victorian heirloom, it's big enough to accommodate a Brother Moodie stretched out full-length. This is where Lou often catches a few winks after she and Grady dine. In the morning, around 4:30, Lou will awaken, slip out, and drive with a clearer head back home. She'll wonder then, as she brakes for a stray mutt crossing the road, if she had enjoyed Cheryl Ames's recital. By the time the mutt is safely across, she will remember what Mrs. Ompala had said during dinner. How Wagner was such a terrible anti-Semite. How the Nazis loved his music. But the Nazis loved Beethoven, too, Lou had put in. And Mozart.

"My dear child," Mrs. Ompala said, "I suppose you like Strauss as well."

"The *Vier Letzte Lieder* are gorgeous. Cheryl is going to sing one of them tonight."

"But that man *was* a Nazi. He was tried by the Allies after the war."

A portobello in her mouth, Grady said, "Richard Strauss was a Nazi? And you want to go hear him, Lou?"

"Well, I . . . What about the sandwiches, the egg salad we made?"

"Bill brought them over to the church yesterday."

"Grady, I really don't think it's right not to go. You made the Arts Council rent Frederik Hall for the recital. And last year, Mrs. Ompala, I was president of the Arts Council. How will it look if we don't show up?"

Without raising her voice or seeming pushy or ungracious, Lou had done her best to get them to go to the recital. She wasn't sure at what point during the dinner she had given up. Perhaps it was when Grady opened a third bottle of Cakebread. And then Bill had had his inspiration and Lou had been pressed into service, helping Grady toss the salad, which Carla, the cook, always served last.

CHAPTER ELEVEN

A lpha has been notified that her services will no longer be required in Brougham Gardens. There will, of course, be no reduction in pay. But from now on, she will only be required to do her domestic engineering at Coffee Ridge.

With her hangover, Lou didn't feel capable of relaying this in person—or on the phone. She composed a letter in the toolshed as soon as she got home from Grady's. It was carefully worded—and took even longer than her Bassoon Society column to write.

Later that same day, after faxing the letter from the office, Lou proposes to Don that he move back to Brougham Gardens. They could rent his parents' house to Mrs. Ompala—on a nominal basis, of course. Whatever the woman could afford.

Don claims he can't wait to move back in with Lou. His parents' house is getting him down, making him think too much about the old days. And he hates the window air conditioners, the noise they make. Lou doesn't realize how good she has it with central air. In the meantime, though, it would be impossible to ask Mrs. Ompala to pay for her room and board. The woman, you see, has no ready funds. Her late husband left her very little to cover his debts, and the will is still being probated. The pecan plantation has been taken over by Mrs. Ompala's sister-in-law. Mr. Ompala had apparently lived on a lavish scale, spending far more than he earned.

"Ompala is such a beautiful name," Lou muses aloud. "I wonder if it means anything in Swahili or . . ."

"No, babe, it's Boer."

"Huh?"

"It's a corruption of a Boer name."

"That's odd. I thought the Boers were in South Africa, not Kenya."

"Right, South Africa, that's where he was from. Then he moved to Mombasa. A regular Clark Gable, that's what Mrs. Ompala said. Same ears."

Lou wonders a moment about Gable.

"You O.K., babe?"

"Fine." She gives his hand a squeeze, firmer than intended. In the glider on the sunporch in Coffee Ridge, they swing gently enough not to disturb the steaming mug cradled between his legs. "It's just that I never imagined him like Gable, more like . . ."

"What? Leslie Howard?"

Lou betrays no surprise, though her disappointment is fierce. All the revisions this entails—the entire story in ruins now. And after she's blabbed everything she thought was true to Grady! Why oh why couldn't Mrs. Ompala have told her this herself? Needing something now, right now, she grabs the mug from between her husband's legs.

"That's *real*," he protests. "Let me get you some decaf."

"Never mind, Don." One sip and it's there again, that lump in her chest. She'll have to get some more heartburn medicine at Rite-Aid. If only she had time to make an appointment with that doctor near the mall in Eutaw, she could get herself prescription strength. That might do the trick.

"What's eating you?"

"I'm fine, Don."

"Rough day at the office?"

"I *said* I'm fine."

He shrugs. "I'm just trying to explain why I can't move out quite yet. We've really got to get Mrs. Ompala settled first."

"Why has this woman suddenly become our problem? I'm sorry she's a little hard up now, Don. But Alpha could be making more of an effort to find her a place. And speaking of Alpha, if Mr. Ompala is a Boer . . ." Boers were some of the worst racists on earth. To think she and Don have been harboring the widow of a Boer, a Mississippi Boer at that. "I mean, is Alpha adopted or what?"

He takes a thoughtful sip from his mug. "Not something she wants discussed, babe. I never asked her myself, but then I found out the other day that whole Oxford business."

"What business, the pecans?"

"No, this was England, Magdalen College. Way back when she was a girl doing some research for her uncle, that bishop. She met a student in the library, a young fella from Rhodesia. Royalty, he was grandson of a tribal queen, so of course she falls head over heels for him—really flips. Wanted to marry him, but his family wouldn't hear of it. Much less her own. Then when she found herself pregnant, that's when the bishop instituted proceedings for statutory rape. She was seventeen, her boyfriend eighteen. He disappeared before he could be arrested, fled the country. She herself was sent away to the bishop's sister in Mombasa. There was no way she could have the child in Worcestershire, of course. Her aunt, Lady Something-or-other . . ."

"Fitzhoward?"

"Yeah, she was the one who found Mr. Ompala for her. Gave him a coffee plantation to manage in the highlands near Nairobi. That's where he made enough to leave Africa, and settle in Mississippi."

"What about Alpha?"

"She was raised on the coffee plantation, adopted by the cook, a Kikuyu. Always believed the cook was her mother. That's how they arranged things."

"It must have been a shock for Alpha—I mean when she found out her real mother . . ."

"That's the whole trouble now—Alpha. You know, of course, what Alpha thinks of the whole thing. It's a shame, isn't it?"

Lou studies her sensible pumps, so comfortable and dowdy. The alligator spike heels Don gave her for her birthday can't be worn as everyday shoes. They hurt, even though the bunion was removed. But a phantom bunion remains, more painful than ever. Of course, the doctors just scoffed at this, wouldn't believe her . . .

"Lou? What's with you, babe?"

She pushes away his hand, which returns to wipe away a tear. "It's so silly, Don. I really don't know why it hurts so much."

"I told you, hon, those shoes aren't good for your arch, not enough support."

"I'm talking about Alpha. She hasn't told me a thing about how she feels. And Mrs. Ompala—I always thought her husband was black. I didn't know the first thing about Oxford or that cook in Africa . . ."

"Shhh. Not so loud."

Alpha was mopping in the kitchen, her shadow passing over the curtained door leading to the in-laws' sunporch.

"So what does Alpha think?" Lou says.

"She never told me herself. I just heard, though, the other day—the whole problem with this apartment issue, getting Mrs. Ompala settled—well, it seems Alpha has too many doubts about Mrs. Ompala. She finds it hard to believe she's really her mother. She thinks Mrs. Ompala is a little senile. Not lying, just deluded."

"But why would Mrs. Ompala make up such a thing?"

"The shock of her husband's death, finding out he was in terrible debt, no one to fall back on, no children to help out—I mean, they had no children themselves, Mr. and Mrs. Ompala."

"Nonsense. Mrs. Ompala is the sanest person I know. She's the only one who sees what a great marriage we have, Don. And if Alpha didn't tell you all this, then how in the world did you . . . ?"

"Shhh."

On the other side of the French doors, Alpha looms. The sheer curtains over the door panes ripple.

"Don," she whispers, "did you give her the fax I sent? Is she mad at me? You'll explain, won't you? I'm doing her a favor. I . . ."

"Shhh."

In the kitchen voices are raised. Alpha takes an awkward step or two. Someone is clutching onto her, a girl, a neighbor's child? No, it must be Mrs. Ompala. But she looks more like a child, so frail, as if *Alpha* were the mother. Not that Alpha is that big, by any means. Lou just never realized before how substantial she is.

Don's grip on her wrist tightens. The curtains frustrate a clear view of the embrace on the other side, yet Lou sees enough to forget the heartburn plaguing her. Or maybe it's the painful pressure on her wrist, working like shiatsu, one ache cured by another.

CHAPTER TWELVE

Painted turtles, gerbils, and roasted cashews once gave Sonny Boy its own peculiar musk, both enticing and repulsive. Taken over by a chain now, the store has an antiseptic aura, featuring a display of generic bleach where the candy counter used to be. No faint chirps from dyed lovebirds distract Lou in her quest for the right shade of blue. As she tries to decide between SeabiscuitAzure and Sunami, something furry alights on her neck. The little screech Lou lets out is so tame that the trainee pricing welcome mats nearby doesn't even look up.

"No, he's not *making* me," Lou says, after explaining to Grady, who's dangling a furred mule in her hand, about the handicapped parking space.

"But I heard Brother Moodie order you to go out and get a can of paint right away. You shouldn't let him talk to you like that."

Lou sighs. Brother Moodie had not yelled at her. He was reminding her, just as Grady was leaving her aerobics class, that the deadline for turning the white space blue was today. Otherwise, the superintendent would issue a substantial fine.

"Why should *you* have to buy paint? Is that a receptionist's job?"

"Grady, it's my fault to begin with. Brother Moodie has been

very patient with me. He's asked me several times to get the paint,
but I had a doctor's appointment last week, which I had to cancel
because my column was . . ."

"Like this?" Grady holds up the turquoise mule. "Only $3.95
and it's a hundred-percent natural. Genuine fitch."

"It's made out of birds?"

"Polecat. Well, got to go find its mate, child. 'Bye."

As Lou pays for the Seabiscuit, she tries not to notice that
Burma Van Buren, the store manager, is crawling around the window display with someone. The someone is Maigrite's husband,
who is rearranging a stack of brake fluid. Mrs. Van Buren keeps on
changing Mr. Pickens's pyramid back into a straight line while ad-
ministering little slaps to his hand.

Outside Freds, Lou lingers a moment as if pondering the mer-
its of this fluid.

"Lunch?"

It's Grady. She's inserted herself between Lou and the pyramid.

"Lunch?" Lou says. "It's ten o'clock."

"Me hungry."

Lou cranes her neck for a better view of the shifting pyramid.
But from this angle, a reflection in the display window blocks the
superintendent's dalliance. An old biddy gazes back at Lou, so like
the home ec teacher she and Grady used to mock. Lou tries not to
look . . .

"Come on," Grady says.

In high school, Lou had been known for her figure. Tall, lithe,
yet buxom, she turned heads. And cried when the football team
elected her, in a secret poll, Most Stacked. She used to make Don
swear, when they were dating, that he didn't care if she was stacked
or not, that it was her mind, not her body . . .

"What are you gaping at, Lou? Come on. Let's get some grub."

She turns away from the plate glass. "I've got to get back to
the office, Grady. If those lines aren't painted blue by this afternoon . . ."

Lou crosses the street at a slight angle, the gallon of blue making her list. In the sunflowers bordering the rusted, misaligned

railroad tracks, Grady brushes Lou's shoulder. "You sleeping with him, is that it?"

"Go home."

"Is this why you don't mind playing Stepin Fetchit for Brother Moodie?"

A swell of bitter hatred propels Lou through the sunflowers. It's not localized, this hatred, though some of it does taint Grady. And Brother Moodie, for rejecting her. For knowing her need, her loneliness.

Lou pries off the lid in the parking lot. She loves Don. She really does. Why isn't this enough?

"So am I right, Lou? Does this explain why you're wasting your life playing janitor for these Jesus freaks?"

Lou slaps a paintbrush into Grady's hand. "I work here because we need the money. In case you forgot, my husband is out of a job. We have a heavy mortgage to pay off and . . ."

"Take it easy, girl."

Lou blows her nose. She's gotten a little moist over the accusation.

"I'd rather you were having an affair with him, Bear. Really."

"Than what?"

"Well, you know, Brother Moodie reminds me of those smarmy preachers who . . ." Grady gestures toward the railroad station. "Just promise me you won't start drinking Kool-Aid someday."

"Someday? How about right this minute? Bring it on, girl."

Grady coughs out a laugh. Sticky as fudge, the asphalt bakes in the sun. The Seabiscuit blue, a discontinued shade, streaks unevenly over the hot glaze, its fumes turning Lou's stomach. Yet she's giggling, as if she and Grady were back in home ec, dizzy with boredom, stale air, the correct way to grease a pan, while Miss Porter, a gardenia wilting on her lace jabot, warns, "Now, gulls, let's cut that out . . ."

They've finished the stylized wheelchair. It's blue again, though not quite the official blue Lou had hoped for, but somewhat green.

Grady touches up one of the boundary lines. She's done most of the work herself, mainly because she's wearing khakis. Lou, in a taupe pantsuit and silk blouse from Saks, stirred the paint from time to time.

Palmetto fronds shiver beneath the tung tree. Lou savors the delicious breeze, coming out of nowhere. "Let me finish up, Grady."

"Get off the goddam wheelchair."

"I'm not on it," Lou says lamely, backing off the wet paint.

Grady's lank mop of hair, normally a dull blond, glistens like silver at this angle, with her head cocked.

"I think I would've died if I had to do it all myself, Miss Morgen. You saved my life."

Lou spits on her lace handkerchief and begins to dab Grady's forehead.

"Stop that."

"You got paint."

Grady yanks away the handkerchief and . . .

"Ladies."

Lou swivels. In a maroon warmup suit, Brother Moodie stands astride the wheelchair, surveying their handiwork.

"I better be going," Grady says to Lou.

"This is blue?" he asks as Grady heads for the sunflowers.

Lou resists an urge to hug him. Nothing sexual about this, of course. More like surrendering to the gravity large bodies exert over smaller—like an asteroid hurtling toward a blessed annihilation.

"Yes, it's blue."

With a grunt, he heads for his Cadillac. She stoops to press the lid back on the can.

The Rabbit needs a new ignition switch. While it's at Mustafa's body shop on Martin Luther King Jr. Road, Lou must ask Maigrite to cover for her. She has to leave early in order to let Don have the BMW for a job interview.

"Why didn't he just drive you to work this morning?" Maigrite asks.

"He didn't discover the Rabbit wouldn't start until a few minutes ago."

"Oh, all right, Louise. Go."

Lou hesitates as Maigrite cascades one window after another on her monitor. Payroll checks fly past.

"Maigrite, I wasn't going to say this, but you know when I went to get the paint this morning, over at Freds, well . . ."

"Well, what?"

"Nothing."

"You saw the superintendent? Helping Burma with the display?" Social Security numbers whiz by. "Is that it? Just quit your worrying, Lou. They're not going to sue you."

"But, Maigrite, all that time Burma and he spend together. I mean, shouldn't your husband be over at City Hall supervising something?"

"It's Flag Day. Mr. Pickens always takes Flag Day off."

"But that's in June, isn't it?"

"*State* flag."

Lou looks at the Piaget on her wrist. "Oh, I see. Well, I better get going."

CHAPTER THIRTEEN

Don asks if she's buckled up properly. Lou asks what he means by "properly." All she knows is that it's buckled. He reaches over and yanks on her seat belt. "Heavenly days," she mutters as the engine turns over.

Lou's out of Liquid Paper, which is impossible to find in Tula Springs, so she's going along to provide moral support. He'd rather be alone, he said, so he could psych himself up for the interview with a motivational tape, *Swim with the Sharks*. That he'd prefer a shark's company to her own, Lou refuses to believe. That's why she got in the car.

"By the way, Lou, there's something I've been meaning to tell you." One finger on the wheel, he backs the BMW out the drive. "All those things I found out about Mrs. Ompala, the rape and all, she didn't tell me herself. So don't go repeating . . . O.K., O.K. I know you won't. Anyway, it was the cook."

"What cook?"

"You know, Grady's. Alpha asked her and that butler over to dinner the other night and . . ."

"What? Don, this is going too far. The entire town is dining with that woman—and not once has she offered me so much as a sardine."

"Babe, you don't give sardines to someone who just fired you."

"Fired? I cut Alpha's workload in half, that's what I did. So she could have time to study and run her Caucus. And this is the thanks I get. I never . . ." With a sudden smile, Lou waves to Mayor Tyde, who's trimming his driveway with a weed whacker. He doesn't wave back, probably because of a glare on the windshield. People inside cars can often be invisible, Lou reassures herself.

"What possible reason could Alpha have had to ask Grady's help over?"

Lou switches off the tape Don had inserted when she wasn't looking. "Don?"

"Huh? Oh, something about the provost. They're helping Alpha get rid of Rowena Cobb at St. Jude because she hired this unqualified man as dean of resource management instead of that Filipino woman from Stanford."

"Wonderful. Wait until Mayor Tyde hears that you're holding meetings to oust the provost because she hired the first African-American dean St. Jude has ever had."

"African-American?"

"Didn't they tell you, Don? Not only that, Dean Whitney is one of Mayor Tyde's best friends. They went to the same school in Alabama."

"God Almighty—the toolshed! I just wrote Mayor Tyde about the toolshed."

"Is that all you can worry about—that toolshed? My Lord, Don, how do you expect to land a job around here if everyone thinks you're a racist?"

"*I'm* not the one trying to get rid of Rowena."

"Maybe not. But the ringleader happens to work for you. Everyone knows Alpha's your housekeeper."

"So? Can't she have a life of her own?"

"You're shacked up with her mother. How do you think that looks? Then you let all these perfect strangers into the house to start agitating . . . What do you know about that cook, anyway? I've always thought it was so strange, someone from the Bronx working for Grady."

"What am I supposed to do? Tell Alpha her friends aren't welcome in my house—our . . . My folks' house. Anyway, Carla told me she used to be Bill's teacher at Yale—a course in Blake, Wordsworth . . ."

"Bill the butler?"

"She didn't get tenure. So Bill the butler invited her to Grady's so she can finish her book on postcolonial infomercials."

"For heaven's sake. It's a writers' colony. All this butler-cook business is just a front. Grady's been . . . Stop!"

The tires squeal as Blue, a hefty Angora, continues his stroll down the middle of the street, unfazed by Don's curses, how this dadblame idiot will make him late for his appointment, cost him a goldang job . . . "I swear if I ever find out who owns that thing . . ."

"Get over it, Don. It's just a cat."

A mile later Don promises to have a talk with Alpha. He'll tell her that she must leave the provost alone, let her be. Enough with all these politics. That's not why she's going to school.

Appealing for some sort of help, Lou casts her eyes up to the heavens—in this case, the BMW's ceiling. Three or four ladybugs are crawling along a seam. "Lord, no, Don, you can't say that to her. All I meant was that she shouldn't use your house to . . . This is all your mother's fault. I never wanted a maid in the first place and now . . ."

"Leave my mother out of this, Lou." He slaps his freckled pate, where a ladybug has landed.

"Don, you simply must find Alpha another job somewhere."

"Yeah, fire her. That would look great, wouldn't it?" Another slap.

"A good job, I mean. Get her a real good job in computers."

"Look, I can't even get myself a job. How am I supposed to . . . ?"

With a sigh, Lou folds her hands in her lap. "Dear, will you please stop killing those ladybugs?"

"They're flying in my face."

"Of all people you should know how good they are. Father always called them *Marienkäfer*. You know what that means?"

"Frankly, my dear, I don't give a damn."

"In France, they're *les vaches de la Vierge*. They eat things that are bad for plants."

"I don't believe there are any aphids in the car."

"Open your window. Just let those little cows fly out, dear. Now what? What are you doing?"

"Counting the spots. Tells you whether they're *Adalia bipunctata* or . . ."

A Saturn pulls out of the Piggly Wiggly warehouse and starts to cut right into their lane. Without looking up from the Virgin's *vache* pinched between his fingers, Don manages to swerve onto the shoulder, avoiding a collision by an inch or two. Lou's scream, *Watch out!* is stillborn, utterly silent.

On the edge of a field rimmed with skinny, listing pines, Mawmaw's Country Store comes into view. Lou's always viewed this establishment with a certain grain of salt. A real country store wouldn't call itself a country store. And the logs look a little too trim and neat.

Don flicks on the turn signal, saying that he wants to stop for gas. But Lou urges him on. She will not get gas at Mawmaw's. Whether it's authentic redneck or a tourist trap, it will be too pricey. Anyway, Lou feels they should wait for a Texaco, because of the opera. Not that she approves of advertising—even underwriting is suspect. But how else would people ever get a chance to hear the more difficult masterpieces? "Like *Moses und Aron*. To tell you the truth, Don, I thought the Houston Opera could have been much more imaginative with Schoenberg, their staging. I was hoping they'd make Moses an illegal alien wandering in from Mexico. He sees Houston and declares God has given this Canaan back to his people."

"Have you seen my golf socks? You have them over at your house, don't you?"

"*My* house? Mister, that fancy joint is *your* house, not mine. I never wanted to live all wired up with . . . Just this morning I set

off the bedroom alarm and . . . Watch that dog. You really have to
come back to Brougham Gardens, Don. I can't have you mixed up
anymore with Alpha's little cabal. Coffee Ridge is getting a reputation."

"I've asked you not to wear my golf socks, Lou."

With a sigh, she pulls down the BMW's visor to shade her eyes.
FREE HBO & VIDE-O! POKER, a sign tall as a water tower proclaims to
the weary. "They're actually *my* socks, Don. I put a special mark on
the heels. Oh, for heaven's sake . . ."

The vanity mirror on the visor reflects a smudge of Seabiscuit
blue on her cheek. Neither Grady, Brother Moodie, nor Maigrite
said a word to her about it. "Wonderful, Don, here I am looking
like a clown and you don't even . . ."

"Here." He hands her an antibacterial wipe.

They pass a body shop, then a cemetery sculpture outlet with
slightly used angels. This is how everyone knows they've entered
Liberty, by the angels leached by age and lichen. There's no sign
for the town, just a single stoplight. Here, waiting for green, Lou
punches off the shark tape again. "I wonder how Alpha got to know
Grady's cook. It seems so odd. It wasn't you, Don, was it?"

"Me what? Carla drove Mrs. Ompala home after Grady's dinner—she and Bill did. Alpha was still there and they got to talking
and I wish you'd let me listen to that tape, Lou."

The light has changed, but the battered pickup in front of them
doesn't move. Don honks. "Asshole! Wake the hell up, grandma!
You want me to lose my job?"

"Don."

"These hicks shouldn't have a license." With the horn still blar-
ing, he swerves around the truck, loaded down in back with a mud-
caked four-wheeler. When Don gives the finger in the rearview
mirror, Lou cranes her neck to see the driver, which turns out to be
a thickset man. If it had been a woman behind the wheel, Lou
would have made a fuss. But she's too weary to defend a cracker
with a rebel flag decal.

"So, you just invite everyone in," Lou says after he's made up for the light by going eighty-six for a few miles. "Carla, Bill, come on in, meet my maid. And what was Alpha doing at Coffee Ridge so late anyway?"

One finger on the wheel, he shrugs. "Look, babe, don't try to put this one on me. Alpha had to use my computer for a paper on the Federal Reserve. I was minding my own business, fixing up your CV . . ."

"*My* CV?"

"They've got an opening at St. Jude, you know. For an assistant professor, tenure track, benefits, and only a three-two load. Alpha found it posted on the Net."

"Alpha? What business does Alpha have meddling in my . . . The nerve."

"Look, Lou, everyone knows it's high time you got out of that WaistWatch racket. You're too good for those bozos. And I've been hearing things, kid. People say things go on there."

"Things? Oh, darn, I was hoping you wouldn't find out about our orgies."

"Go ahead, laugh. But something's fishy about the place." He passes an Explorer whose driver is chatting on the phone. "All those sexpots in Lycra working out with Jesus."

"You been talking to Grady?"

"How could I? Wasn't me invited to her fancy dinner party."

Lou asks him to slow down. Then: "You said yourself you didn't have time. Anyway, you wouldn't have wanted to go to a hen party."

In a copse of slash pines a squad car lurks, but Don doesn't bother to slow down. He tells Lou it's a dummy inside the car. Saves the parish a lot of money, using a dummy.

As they whiz past, Lou gets a glimpse of platinum Barbie-like hair and pouting red lips. Probably a discontinued mannequin, something that no decent store would be caught dead with today.

By the time they find the yacht club in Ozone, Lou's annoyance with Don has fizzled, gone flat, despite her attempts to give it a good shake from time to time. After all, he couldn't help it if Alpha told him about that music theory job at St. Jude. And it was Mrs. Ompala, not Don, who had invited the butler and cook into the house for a nightcap.

"Pray for me, babe." His brown eyes, dark as a gypsy's, plead. Lou knows how important this interview is to him. He's having drinks with a vice president of MaxCo here at the St. Jude Yacht Club, an establishment Lou can't really approve of. Refugees from New Orleans make up the bulk of the membership, old farts and yuppies who'd fled from the rising crime rate across Lake Pontchartrain. They'd gentrified the entire North Shore, raising property values in a ripple effect as far north as Tula Springs. If Lou had the power, she'd deport them all back to the city, where they could learn to get along with their fellow citizens. In any case, she keeps her disapproval to herself this afternoon. She's not going to put a damper on his big day. Already Don's had three successful interviews with MaxCo executives, who've narrowed the field to three candidates. It's possible Don might even get an offer over drinks.

Lou strokes the crew cut that he promised to let grow out. It's two-toned now, gray at the roots. He's given up Grecian Formula, as well. In return, she's promised to wear his birthday present— stiletto mules—the next time she sleeps over at Coffee Ridge.

"How can anyone turn you down, Donnie boy?" She squeezes a dab of WW ProPhysique into the crew cut. "Hold still, Mister. There. Not bad. You know, Don, that two-tone effect, it's sort of cool. Especially with these shades. Put them on."

Bill the butler had left behind his $300 sunglasses at Coffee Ridge when he had driven Mrs. Ompala home. Lou plans to return them to Grady tomorrow.

"I can't wear these."

"Go on. Get out. And don't look so stiff when you walk. Pretend you've gotten over The Citadel."

As he strides down the pier, he reverts to military posture. Not quite average height, he believes he has to hold himself more rigid than other men. Lou smiles. From a distance now, he could be a teenager, awkward and lean in his first real suit. Without telling Don, Lou had consulted Lynda at WaistWatch about his wardrobe.

It was she who had suggested a more generous cut to his suits. And a label that cost half what Armani would, yet looked pretty much the same. He hated the suit at first, said it made him look like a don. But he's wearing it nonetheless—as well as the shoes she bought to replace his tasseled loafers. Lynda said men should never wear tassels.

"I'll be back at six!" she calls to him. "Got to go get my Liquid Paper now!"

A brown gull swoops for an oyster it has dropped, purposely, onto the deck of a cigarette boat. Don pauses a moment to watch the gull dine, then marches on.

CHAPTER FOURTEEN

Grady unwraps the aluminum foil. Sauerkraut leaks through the homemade rye. Stacked perilously high, the leaning tower of pastrami threatens to collapse onto Lou's carefully penned log of incoming and outgoing phone calls.

"Not here," Lou says. "Not at my desk, please, Ma'am."

In gray sweatpants and a T-shirt borrowed from a Sherpa, Grady unzips a plastic bag stuffed with a flabby blini. "Where's the microwave?"

"Grady, I told you we can't eat at my desk."

"Why not? Brother Moodie eats at his. Lynda, I've seen her eat in her office. Pickle?"

Lou waves away the huge kosher dill.

"Georgia, LaTonya, Tifawni—they all eat in their office."

"This is not an office. This is a reception area. How do you suppose it'll look if a new customer comes in and sees all this grease . . . Oh, hi, Maigrite."

Malgrite has emerged from Lynda's office. A slim Gucci portfolio under her arm, Maigrite smiles at Grady, who nods back, speechless. She's bitten off half the dill and can only munch.

Maigrite informs Lou that Lynda wants to review yesterday's log. Lou hands her the sheet.

"Not September. Yesterday's."

"This is yesterday's," Lou says, crossing out *September*. She writes in *December*. "I had to get up at four-thirty this morning, you know, my bassoon column. I'm just exhausted and . . . Anyway . . ."

As Maigrite returns to Lynda's office, Grady says something unintelligible while crunching the pickle. Lou knows it's a crack about Maigrite. Maybe a remark about the sleighs on her sweater. Or the heels pitched so steeply, she actually totters.

"Yes, it was good," Lou admits after finishing half of the Reuben. They're eating in the BMW right outside the railroad station. It's warm enough to keep both doors open for a breeze. Was it really any wonder that for a moment, she might have thought it was September? At her age, without dependable, clear-cut seasons, she shouldn't be blamed for an occasional slip. Especially after such a morning. She had awoken with heartburn so bad that she had been forced to dose her orange juice with a touch of vodka. Yes, she should definitely get a checkup soon. But she couldn't go to any of the doctors Don had sued. And that doctor she had tried out in Ozone wasn't a bit of help. He refused to renew the old, pre-bunion sleeping pill prescription and warned her sternly about the herbal diet pills from WaistWatch that she used whenever she felt tired. Now she had to use her Gibsons to get to sleep. Well, it was a shame WaistWatch employee insurance only covered those doctors at the Pentecostal hospital. Out of the question, of course. She wouldn't be examined by someone speaking in tongues.

"Tell Carla thanks," Lou says. "Great Reuben."

"She didn't make this. It was me, girl." Grady takes a swig of seltzer. "Carla doesn't have time to cook anymore. She's on a roll with her postcolonial book."

Lou plucks a bit of Swiss cheese from the seat and samples it. "Seems to me she has plenty of time to spare for Alpha's campaign. I wish they'd stop persecuting Rowena. Did you see that op-ed piece in the paper yesterday? It's a disgrace."

"Carla didn't write that. That was Alpha—with a little help from Bill."

"How was Rowena supposed to know what Dr. Whitney did as a freshman in college? So what if he was a little conservative back then and denounced Stokely Carmichael? You'd be careful, too, if you were living in Alabama back then."

"I was in Mississippi, even worse."

"And you were the oppressor, Grady. Don't ever forget."

"Thanks, Bear. I'll make a note of it."

Nine robins have alighted on the roof of Brother Moodie's Cadillac. They jockey for position, pecking at drops from a recent downpour. In the nearly bare limbs of the tungs, scores of them exult. Some plunge to the hood while others flutter up from the gleaming roof to the few sere leaves. Lost in wonder at their horny feet, so stark a contrast to their downy breasts, Lou forgets her comeback. Birds really don't look natural at all, she realizes. More like some mythological hybrid.

"I just hate to see my name get mixed up in all this," Lou says. "Don and I both support Rowena's decision. I've written her a note, you know. Lord, what a job she must have. You couldn't pay me a million a year to be provost. One good thing, though. She's got the African-American faculty and students on her side. They're pro Dean Whitney."

"But NOW is supporting Alpha."

"What?"

"Just heard it from the horse's mouth. The St. Jude chapter of NOW is campaigning for Dr. Gloria Luz Smith to replace Rowena."

"The horse's mouth? But you're president of NOW. How could you do this to a friend?" Lou sets aside the Reuben.

"You going to eat this?" Grady picks up the sandwich.

"Go ahead."

Lou peers quizzically as Grady tries hard to swallow the pastrami. Always biting off more than she can chew, mainly to spite her mother, who believed that a young lady must never put more than a taste in her mouth. And must never seem to enjoy it.

Grady squints with the effort. It finally goes down. "I voted for Rowena. But it's a democracy, Bear. The other girls overruled me."

"What about my vote? I haven't voted yet."

"No, and you haven't paid your dues either. Or attended the last five sessions."

"Well, I had to do the color commentary on the Christmas parade, you know, and the raffle for B'nai B'rith was . . ." Something catches Lou's eye. "On the dashboard, Grady. Look. I've been meaning to give those back to you."

Grady moans, massaging her thigh. "That rapping nearly killed us today . . . What? These?" She holds up the sunglasses. "These aren't mine."

Lou gets out of the car. "I know. Bill left them at Coffee Ridge some time ago. And I keep on forgetting to bring them back. Put them in your purse right now. I don't want them on my conscience any longer."

As she heads for the train station, Lou frowns at a curious bleat. It's her own horn, the BMW's.

"You got to take me to Alpha's!" Grady yells, sticking her head out the window. "I need to get my car."

"Walk."

"Last time I walked, I was picked up and questioned by Our Miss Turd's patrol. This town ain't made for walking, girl."

"You've really got to stop letting Carla use your car all the time. Why can't she ride with Bill?"

"Come on, Lou. Don't try to teach me any lessons now."

As Lou stands there, wondering why she has to be inconvenienced by Grady's rash and inappropriate generosity, Lynda's Cougar pulls into the lot. The BMW, Lou remembers now, is in Lynda's parking space. Stuffed into the front seat of the Cougar, Lynda, Tifawni, and LaTonya wave to Lou as she heads back to the BMW. She's going to have to give up the space.

"God, I hate them," Grady mutters as Lou brakes for the three young women, bronze and full of grace. Lou has the right of way, but they stride directly in front of the BMW. Lynda has parked in the handicapped space, rather than wait for the BMW to move. "Have you ever seen such asses, Lou?"

"Well, they may not be the brightest of God's creatures, parking in a handicapped space after all the trouble we've had with City Hall, but you shouldn't ever say . . ."

"I'm talking about their *butts*. If I had an ass like that, oh, baby . . . I'd have me such a good ole hubby. Come on, Bear. Go."

Two miles from the train station, Coffee Ridge had once been outside the city limits. Houses here were much less expensive than comparable homes in Tula Springs itself. No one wanted to send their children to the parish school. But since it had been swallowed up by the town, Coffee Ridge prices had jumped a good 30 to 40 percent. Maybe even more because it was so close to the Wal-Mart Super Store, where you could buy quail eggs, bank, and get your hair permed all under one roof. Don Sr. and Maybelle had bought their three-bedroom house for a song back in 1949. What it must be worth now, Lou would rather not know.

"Want to come in?" Grady says as Lou pulls into the driveway.

Lou shakes her head. With the engine running, she suffers a pang of admiration. This wood-frame house, in need of paint, is real. Its modest, gentle nooks and crannies blend perfectly with the yard. The glorious azaleas—Gulf Pride, Formosa, Christmas Cheer, Flame, Peach Blow—will in six weeks or so magnify the lawn Maybelle slaved over, the clash of crimson, lavender, and peach creating, as a maze does, space within space. Only time, slow painful years, can landscape like this, lacing the cedar and sweet gums into a seamless canopy over the bed of gardenias. Brougham Gardens—with its $350,000 homes—seems like a project in comparison.

"What's wrong?" Grady asks.

Lou sighs. "Are you getting out of the car or not?"

Reaching over, Grady turns off the ignition. "Not until you spit it out."

"I've got to get back to work." Lou doesn't start the engine, though. A cardinal perched on a sagging limb of a water oak cries out lustily. Maybelle used to fret about this limb, saying she just knew it was going to come crashing down someday, headed right for Don Sr.'s bald spot as he dozed in his La-Z-Boy.

"Why can't you be glad for her?" Grady says.

"Who? Alpha? I'm glad."

"She's worked all her life for Maybelle. Don't you think she deserves a little reward?"

"Look, I've told you before I'm glad. I'm very happy for Alpha."

Maybelle and Don Sr. had died within a few weeks of each other, back in October. Being the last to go, Maybelle not only left the house in Coffee Ridge to Alpha, but also over a quarter million in their retirement fund. Don, who hadn't wanted his parents to worry about him, had led them to believe he was more than well-off, and that he had gotten the MaxCo job paying 175 grand a year. It wasn't exactly a lie, because at the time, just before his parents died, he was one of two finalists. After his mother's funeral, though, he found out the job went to a younger man from Seattle. Since then, Alpha had given up her own apartment and moved into Coffee Ridge.

Grady kneads her shoulder. "Bear, don't you think it's pretty cool? I mean, all these years you thought Maybelle was a racist. And here she leaves practically everything to her maid."

"Are you kidding?"

Grady winces as she rubs her thigh. "Brother Moodie nearly killed us today. I'll never be able to take up my pallet and walk."

"Grady, you're joking about Maybelle, aren't you?"

"Well, the old bat doesn't seem as bad as you made her out to be."

Lou starts the engine. "Look, the only reason she left Alpha almost everything was because of me. To spite *me*."

"Poor little legs . . . Ohhh."

"I'm not kidding. She knew exactly what she was doing. She never forgave Don for marrying a Jew."

"A Christian, Bear. That's what he married."

"A Jew. I'm a Jew—nothing will ever change that. As far as that goes, Maybelle and I see eye to eye."

"Give me a break."

Her yawn, Grady's, is like a silent scream. Lou stares for a moment, somewhat fascinated, before going on.

"It's not really about religion anyway, Grady. That woman was a racist, plain and simple. She said *colored* all the time. And she loved to spout off about all the women and children working sixteen hours a day in abolitionists' mills up North. For heaven's sake, she actually believed George Wallace was sorry for what he did. And she once had this Jackie Kennedy pillbox made out of a Confederate flag."

"Are you going to finish this?" Grady says, holding up a partially gnawed blintz.

"Go ahead. How can I eat anything? It makes me ill that anyone can actually think Maybelle's some sort of great liberal benefactor."

Grady squints, swallows. "Lou, you got to admit. I mean, if Maybelle really were as racist as you say, it's sort of self-defeating, giving everything to Alpha just to spite you. To do all that out of hate, I mean, it just doesn't make sense. Don is her only child, after all."

"I told you, she thought Don didn't need the house or the money. She thought we were sitting pretty."

"You want to know something, girlie?" Grady wads up the foil speckled with sour cream. "You're not sounding very Christian, if you ask me."

"Who's asking?"

"Look, Alpha's worked all her life for peanuts. Now she has a decent home, financial security . . . I don't know, maybe I'm wrong, but if it were me, I'd feel pretty good about my mother-in-law. Anyway, I better scoot."

Grady is halfway up the drive before Lou sees the sunglasses on the dash. She wants to call out to her. But she can't now. She simply can't.

Some other time she'll return Bill's shades.

CHAPTER FIFTEEN

Lou is in the kitchen peeling zest when the alarm goes off. With the lemon still in her hand, she hurries past the pot-belly stove that not only microwaves but can also convect six capons in under an hour. Just as she thought. Don has tried to set the table with the Sèvres china that was on display in the specially rigged whatnot, their most valuable piece of furniture. An authentic Wallace Nutting, the tulipwood cabinet is poised to go off at the slightest touch.

"Now look what you've done."

"I thought you turned it off, babe."

"Why would I turn it off when I told you to use the Spode?"

"You said Sèvres."

"I meant Spode, you should know that." She's frantically punching numbers on the alarm. But the code is eluding her. She's getting it mixed up with the password that secures the doors at WaistWatch.

After a long minute the Wallace Nutting stops whining. It's her father's birthday—12 09 13. That's the code.

Back in the kitchen Lou attaches lemon zest to the rims of two crystal glasses. Admiring her handiwork, she begins to hum. And is still humming when she brings the weighty glasses out on a Tiffany tray garnished with Don's thoughtful gift, an orchid.

Aside from the whatnot and a Shaker dining table, all the major pieces of furniture downstairs in the Brougham Gardens home are built-in. The sofa, a ledge of heart pine, runs like a three-dimensional dado along the length of one wall. Needlepoint cushions soften the bench-like effect, but Don himself never uses them. The bare wood, he claims, is good for his bad back.

"Shouldn't you put that in water?" Don asks as he plucks the orchid from the tray.

"Would you please take your drink?" The tray is heavy. Her arms ache.

"Just a sec."

He gets up and goes to the kitchen, fully visible from the sofa. Like a SoHo loft, the first floor of this Cajun Cabin doesn't define any separate rooms. Lou has never shaken the feeling that she's in some sort of public space, perhaps the lobby of an arts-and-crafts museum. It would have been nice if Don had consulted her before surprising her with this anniversary present seven years ago.

He returns with a Waterford vase lapping water onto the slate floor. In goes the orchid. Now he can pick up his drink.

"Cheers," he says.

Holding up her own glass, Lou smiles. She's put the tray on an extension of the heart pine, which can be used as an end table. Or a perch.

"You know, I think the light is better this way," he says after a sip or two.

She follows his gaze to the skylight, a trapezoid slightly off center.

"Not so harsh. I mean it used to be pretty harsh, Lou, that light. Don't you think?"

He's referring to a recent development in Brougham Gardens. A Cineplex is under construction next door. Their kidney-shaped pool is already shaded by a cinderblock wall three stories high, the back of the Crystal Castle. There will be ten separate theaters with plenty of parking for one and all.

"You're very philosophical about it, Don."

"Well, what else can I do? I tried."

A month ago, when Don had gotten wind of the plans for the Cineplex, he had stormed into Mayor Tyde's office at City Hall. But the damage was already past repair. The zoning board had approved the commercial use of the land within the gated community by a vote of 4 to 3. Last week Don's letter had finally been published in the Tula Springs *Herald*. A bitter denunciation of the zoning board, the letter raised questions about certain members' profits from the sale of the land to the Cineplex corporation, headquartered in Singapore.

"You realize what this place must be worth now, Don? Who's going to want to pay three hundred thousand for a . . ."

"All right, all right."

Hunched over, he contemplates the Gibson's zest.

Lou slides over to him. Awkwardly, she tries to put her arms around him. His back stiffens, his neck. "Please come home, Don. We'll figure out a way to get by."

"It's not right, Lou. Mama had no right."

"You can't stay there any longer. It's really getting embarrassing. I don't know what people are beginning to think. When I dropped Grady off today, at Alpha's . . ."

"Who cares what Miss High and Mighty thinks?"

"Don, Grady's my dearest friend. I know she's worried about us."

"Tell her to mind her own business."

She pulls him toward her, stiff neck and all. Silent, she rocks him gently, her own back strained by the odd angle of his resistance. He's still not recovered from his loss. Don loved his parents terribly, especially Maybelle. When he had refused to move out of the house on Coffee Ridge after the reading of the will, everybody, even Lou, could understand that he needed the comfort of those familiar walls, Maybelle's cows, to tide him over. But it's been two months now. And he's been talking about contesting the will, saying that Maybelle couldn't possibly have meant to leave the house and all that money to Alpha. He's come to think that his mother was suffering from a kind of dementia at the end. A religious fixation that she wouldn't get into heaven because of her racist past. He's told Lou that if he moves out of Coffee Ridge, he'll be conceding that the will is valid. Possession is nine-tenths of the law, and all that sort of thing, which Lou doubts is really the law at all. Of course, with Louisiana's Napoleonic Code, one can't be too sure of anything about the law.

"If you love me, Don, you'll move out. You'll come back home."

"It's an insult to you, Lou. Don't you see? I'm not going to see you insulted. I won't have it."

"Well, if your mother was insulting me, then she couldn't have been demented. You've lost your case."

"No, darling. Just the opposite. If anyone could insult you, it proves they were demented." His tongue outlines the whorls of her ear. "Mama just wouldn't have done something like this to me. She wouldn't hurt me so bad. How could she be in her right mind . . ."

"No, Don, stop . . ."

The tongue probes deeper. If she doesn't pull away, dinner will be ruined. She's got to take the garlic bread out of the steamer—right away. And the chicken marsala Don brought over will be dried out if it convects any longer in the potbelly.

"We'll sell the BMW, Don. That will help out, won't it?" She's arched her back, away from the artful tongue. He tugs at his buckle, turquoise-studded silver, brash as a cowboy's. Seeing his veined hands there, so strong, so sure, she forgets she should be worrying about the food. Even her heartburn seems to be dissolving. And she hasn't even finished her third Gibson yet.

The slate floor is cold, and though dry, feels damp. She wants to move over to the rug, which would be so much more comfortable against her bare flesh. But it was handwoven by a Hopi, and too easily stained. Anyway, there's something about his hot flesh on top, the chill beneath. She just wishes she didn't feel so paranoid about making love in her own home, with her own husband.

"Oh, Don, Don . . ."

"Easy, Louis, easy . . ."

Over his hairy shoulder, Lou sees the front door inch open, just a crack. The wind? No, wind doesn't move so cautiously.

"Don? Don!"

"Go, babe, go!"

A derringer edges in first, probing the shadows of the cavernous space flickered by candlelight.

"Don!" Lou whispers frantically. She gropes wildly for the rug, hoping to cover his naked back. But it's just beyond reach, the Hopi masterpiece. "No, stop," she whispers, giving him a good hard pinch.

"Oooooh, yes, babe, yes . . ."

Desperate, she calls out from the floor, "May I help you?"

Spiked heels clatter against the slate. Then: "Oh, it's you, Mrs. Jones. I thought maybe . . ."

"Do you have to point that at us, Mrs. Tudie? Thank you."

The tax assessor, with a gaze as clinical and indifferent as an ambulance driver's, regards Don as, with a spasm or two, he finally subsides.

"Your alarm went off, Mrs. Jones. We at AAA SecureCare have a contractual obligation to respond immediately. Besides, there's been some weird personnel impacting this neighborhood, you know. Vandalized the Crystal Castle just last night. Took all the A's off the sign."

Lou adjusts Don's naked legs so they cover her spider veins a little better. "Everything's fine, Mrs. Tudie. It was the whatnot, that's all."

Like the sickly petals of a magnolia, the collar of Mrs. Tudie's blouse wilts in limp lush folds beneath her liposuctioned chin. A wrinkle in the vest of her maroon pants suit is smoothed by the derringer's mother-of-pearl.

"Good-bye, Mrs. Tudie," Lou prompts. "Thanks for stopping by."

The hint seems to work. But at the door, the woman pauses: "You see any A's around, Mrs. Jones, we'd like them back. They don't grow on trees, you know, red letters that size."

"Excuse me? Are you insinuating . . ."

"Mrs. Jones, you've already vandalized a parking lot in an attempt to obviate the rights of the disabled." With the derringer, she pats her frosted hair, bulbous as a crash helmet. "O.K., Pickens!" she yells up at the skylight. Her arms semaphore strenuously, like a Singaporan traffic cop's. "All clear!"

A bland round face peering down upon the scene fades away.

Lou keeps staring, as if the face were still there. "Would you mind telling me what that man is doing up on my roof?"

"Moonlighting, Mrs. Jones. We've had to put on extra human resources since the vandalism."

"You mean to say the superintendent has nothing better to do than spy on . . . Don't you know that man hates Charlton Heston?"

"Pickens happens to be family, Mrs. Jones. My first cousin once removed. By the way, we got a special this week. Front-door installation ten percent off. You get that put back in and you won't never have to worry about someone walking in like now. Can't blame me, you know. I told Joe Don there he'd regret having the alarm taken out. Evening, Joe Don."

Long ago, after she had started going steady with him in high school, Lou had lopped off the first part of her husband's name. Hearing it now, she feels a kink in her chest. "Good night, Mrs. Tudie," Lou mutters, slapping down the limp wave from Don to the tax assessor.

"Back door, five percent off. By the way, Joe Don, Melvin thanks you for helping make the Firearms Education Expo such a success. Raised over ten G's."

After the door clicks shut, Don resumes with a fury that almost swallows up Lou's own shame and outrage. But it is not quite enough.

When he's finally done, she isn't.

"I hope you're satisfied, Don. You had to have a house with a skylight, didn't you?"

"Let it go, Lou."

"You never consult me about anything. I could've told you it was a terrible idea. Here. Hook me."

He fastens the bra in back. "The solar panels save us hundreds on electricity, Lou. If you had a head for math, you'd understand these things."

"You want math, then why don't you do as I've asked time and time again? Cancel that idiotic contract with Mrs. Pain in the Neck. I'm sick and tired of being raided every time I bump into a piece of furniture."

"I did cancel. But they give you a grace period on the whatnot before they come and unwire it. Three months or something. Costs so much to reinstall there, very delicate work."

Looking up doubtfully at the skylight, she sighs. "Honestly. There ought to be a law. Everyone in City Hall seems to work for Mrs. Tudie now."

"Well, superintendents don't make that much, Lou. Besides, you can't see in from up there. The solar panels won't allow it. You can only see out."

"Really? Oh, Don, you mean that horrible Pickens didn't see us?"

"Cross my heart. You think I'd install a big peephole like that for my girl? Hey! The chicken."

In black socks, nothing else, he skates over to the kitchen. Upset as she is, she can't help smiling at how childish he can seem. His arms flail, as if for balance on a skateboard.

Yanking support hose over her varicose veins, she says, "The gall of that woman, asking *me* about those damn A's."

"What?"

"Nothing."

CHAPTER SIXTEEN

In the locker room of the country club that once hadn't allowed women to set foot on its greens, Grady putts a wadded-up candy wrapper under a listing card table. With a groan, Lou leans over and picks the trash up. A Payday. She disposes of it properly, in a gallon can that once housed lard.

"Do you realize the men's locker room has Ralph Lauren wastebaskets, a sauna, *and* free hair dryers? Why should you play janitor for a bunch of pigs?"

"It's not the pigs who have to clean up after us."

Lou picks some mud from the cleats of her golf shoes. She and Grady have just placed first in the Mixed Pairs Tournament, which has netted $9,539 for Habitat for Humanity. Grady, who paid a voluntary entry fee of $4,500, was supposed to have been partnered with a man, preferably a husband. But having neither available, she had dragged Lou into the tournament. They were both declared illegal until the tournament's marshal opened Grady's envelope and discovered the size of the check.

"Eighty-nine, girl. Damn."

"Was that my score?" Lou asks, knowing full well it was.

"Beat me by five. And I've been studying my swing for months."

Even though Lou regrets not having confronted Mrs. Tudie on

the fifteenth hole—*What in heaven's name would I want with a red A, Mrs. Tudie?*—she's enjoying her triumph. If she runs into Mrs. Tudie again, she won't be so cowardly. So what if Mrs. Tudie was the tournament marshal? It's all over now. They can't take away her title.

"That bogie on thirteen," Lou prompts, fishing for a compliment, "I really thought my stroke was way off. I should have used a . . ."

Stark naked, Carla Perlmutter emerges from the shower. Lou averts her gaze from the handsome figure, amazingly svelte for a fifty-three-year-old. Indeed, Carla looks so good that Lou suspects her of lying about her age. She must be younger.

Without even bothering to drape a towel around her middle, Carla plops down on the bench beside Lou. "Go ahead. I'm through."

Lou smiles politely. "I always shower at home."

"Can't stand being all sweaty."

"I don't have a towel."

"Here you go." Carla holds out her own.

"Thanks," Grady says, snatching the towel away from her cook. She heads to the one shower with it, saving Lou for the moment. The shower has no stall, no door, and she doesn't care for Carla—or Grady—to see her cellulite.

"How did you and Bill do?" Lou asks.

"Eighty-five for me."

"Oh, my. That's wonderful."

"Wonderful, yes. Bill had a stellar day, one thirty-nine. We came in dead last."

"Well, he's rather young and all," Lou says, buttoning up her sweater a notch. Although it seemed warm enough on the course—for January, at least—it's dank and cold in the locker room. The cinderblock walls are not insulated.

"'And all' is right." Carla brushes her grayish mane vigorously. There's a healthy sheen that reminds Lou of a palomino, an expensive, well-groomed mare not shy of klieg lights.

Feeling trapped by an uncomfortable silence—it might seem

rude to simply walk out—Lou makes a few inane remarks about the weather. And then, as casually as possible: "How's the campaign going?"

A look. That's all Carla gives her, a blank look.

Lou, deserving better, stows her niblick with the other clubs that Maybelle had bestowed on her as a wedding gift. Maybelle had bought herself a brand-new set of clubs and decided that the bride, who despised golf, could stand to develop a more mature attitude toward the sport. Of course, at the time of the wedding, Lou wasn't allowed to play at the country club, so Maybelle taught her a few pointers at the public driving range near the rendering plant.

"What campaign, Lou?"

"To oust the provost. You realize that Rowena Cobb is a dear friend of Grady's."

"Nineteen, twenty, twenty-one . . ." Carla counts the strokes of her hairbrush.

"Why must Rowena be persecuted? Doesn't Alpha realize how this looks—to some people?"

"What do you mean? Twenty-four, twenty-five . . ."

"Well, here she is with a white mother, and she's turning against her own . . . I mean, Dr. Whitney is the first African-American to be appointed as a dean at St. Jude."

"For one thing, Lou, Dean Whitney himself doesn't support affirmative action. Alpha thinks that's wrong. For another, Mrs. Ompala isn't her mother."

"What?"

"Twenty-eight . . . No. Where was I? Anyway, Alpha found out for sure Mrs. Ompala isn't her mother. It was the other cook, the one before Alpha's mother. She's the one who adopted the child. Mrs. O has been . . . confused, let's say. Twenty-one, twenty-two . . ."

"Oh."

"So she's split."

"Who? Mrs. Ompala? But where did she go? I mean, I thought she didn't have anywhere to go—no money, just those in-laws in Mississippi and . . ."

"Hey!" Carla is suddenly on her feet. "My shampoo."

She snatches the bottle from the shower, where Grady is already lathered.

"This stuff costs, Morgen. You use your own cheap shit."

As Carla strides away with her herbal protein, Grady rolls her towel and snaps a rattail at the cook's bare ass. With a hoot, Carla sprints for her locker, elbowing Lou on the way. Accidentally, of course.

"Here," Bill says as Lou wheels Maybelle's golf bag out of the locker room, backward.

Lou takes the ornate trophy from him but keeps her distance. Without a shower, she's a little insecure. Fresh and sleek as an otter, the butler lounges against a phone booth.

Another hoot. A shriek.

"What's going down in there?" He flicks an ash from his cigarette onto the carpet. A red-and-violet tartan, it pads everything in the clubhouse—the foyer, dining room, smoker, men's locker room, the pro shop, janitor's closet—everything but the women's locker room. There the busy pattern finally shuts up.

"Girls will be girls," Lou says, vaguely troubled. She's never seen Grady behave so childishly before.

The butler trails Lou out to the parking lot, where she presses a teal dot on her key ring. It's supposed to open the BMW's trunk, but the hood unlocks instead. Under the young man's gaze, she pretends to examine the engine for a moment, then slams the hood shut.

"Listen, maybe Grady would like this," she says, hugging the trophy to her knit shirt. Her heart skips a beat or two—nothing alarming. After all, she had taken a few WaistWatch diet pills in order to give her the energy to play her best.

"O.K." He reaches for the trophy, which she clutches tighter.

"Of course, I did get the lower score."

"So keep it. I'm sure Miss G. cares."

With her key she unlocks the trunk and tries to heave the clubs inside. But they're too heavy.

"Thanks, Bill."

He's come to the rescue. She studies him a moment as he slams the trunk and flicks his cigarette away. Neither handsome nor ugly, he has the inscrutable self-consciousness of an Occidental playing a Brahmin. His gestures seem deliberate, timed.

"One thirty-nine isn't that bad. Here." She hands him the trophy—or tries to. His pale arms, folded over his skinny chest, remain put.

"Like it's real, Lou."

The Dr. Dre T-shirt that the marshal declared obscene before opening Grady's envelope doesn't seem warm enough for January. Goose bumps stipple his arm.

"The score? Do you think they didn't count your strokes right, Bill?"

From a loudspeaker in the eaves of the Tudor clubhouse, the national anthem, as stylized by James Taylor, seeks some resolution. The butler winces.

"Bill? Or do you mean the trophy?"

Carefully sculpted into cowlicks and uneven spikes, his cropped hair has no gray, Lou suddenly realizes, but has aquired a strand of Spanish moss. She plucks it away, warning him about red bugs.

"How can anyone play a decent game with that woman giving me pointers?"

"I thought it was exceedingly generous of Dr. Cobb to correct your swing, Bill."

"Dr. Cobb? That was the provost? Rowena Cobb?"

"Of course. Here you are trying to ruin her life, run her out of office, and she still offers a helping hand."

He tugs on his brisk goatee. "Cool. More like sabotaged my game."

"Don't be silly." Lou tries to stop looking at the "mOthAh" emblazoned on his drooping T-shirt. "By the way, Carla said Mrs. Ompala has left Coffee Ridge. What does this mean? I'm really worried about her, Bill." Not far away, cattails winnowed by a gust shimmer, yield. "Is it really true Alpha's not her daughter?"

"Yeah."

He's sitting on the asphalt, leaning against her whitewalls. She's not sure how he got there with no apparent transition at all. Probably when she was looking off at the water hazard. How dear those cattails seem, how real in the midst of all this labored, graceless turf.

"See, Lou, Alpha would have to be thirty-nine to be her daughter. And she's not. She's fifty-two."

"Who figured that out?"

"Mrs. O. had the birth certificate. She showed it to Alpha the other night."

Lou squints. The sun has dropped a notch. Filaments of moss on a nearby oak glow like tungsten in a lamp. "But that means Mrs. Ompala is only . . . what? Fifty-seven or so? How is that possible?"

Mary Ellen Shavers, recording secretary of the Colonial Dames, glances curiously at the butler as she eases past in her Saab. Lou must resist a strong urge to ask Bill to rise.

He strokes his goatee. "Well, Mrs. O. never said she was seventy or whatever. We all just assumed . . ."

"No wonder she looks so good, Bill. I always thought it was a miracle." Lou sighs. She still wants to believe, but how can she now? "So what happened? Where did she go?"

"Your husband."

"What?"

"He found a place for her."

"Where? Where did she go?"

He squints up at her, shading his eyes. "You mean you don't know?"

"Of course, I . . . Don and I . . ." Drained, she feels. Totally hungover. And yet she hadn't had a drop yesterday, not even with the heartburn acting up. She wanted to be in top form for the tournament, so she stuck to Percodan to get through the pain.

"I was hoping you'd tell *me,* Lou. I've been worried about her, too."

"Well, anyway . . ."

"You two history, Lou? You and the Donald?"

"His name is Dr. Jones. And no, we happen to be extremely close, and I don't think this is any of your business, young man."

He plucks some mud from his cleats. "Hey, didn't mean to like . . . Just that he's still there. In Alpha's house. Every time we go over to see Alpha, he's like hanging out. Weird."

"What's weird is you, Bill. You and Carla. What are you two going over there for? You have nothing to do with St. Jude. Why should you care whether Rowena—Dr. Cobb—is provost or not? If you and your teacher must throw someone out, go back to Yale and get rid of their administration."

"So you think homophobia is O.K."

"Dr. Cobb is not homophobic."

"She appointed a dean who closed down the St. Jude Gay and Lesbian Student Alliance."

"Well, I . . ."

"And your husband, he told me last night Dean Whitney was right. College students are too young to decide if they're gay or not."

"Look, Don happens to be a very compassionate man, especially when it comes to lesbians. And would you please get up, Bill? Stop leaning against my tire. It looks like there's been an accident." She smiles brightly at a gleaming black Volvo inching by the butler. He accepts her outstretched hand and with a groan, gets to his feet.

"Some compassion, Lou. Everyone knows he threw two lesbians out of that house. Can't believe they never sued him."

"For your information, he happened to think they were heterosexual. That's why he threw them out."

"Yeah, right."

"I swear, Bill. And furthermore, Don himself left The Citadel because of their policy toward lesbians."

"What's The Citadel?"

"Good heavens, don't tell me you don't know the most famous military academy in all . . ."

A couple emerge from the clubhouse—the Cobbs.

Rowena's husband, Crosby, waves at Lou, who snatches open the door of the BMW. She doesn't want to talk to them now, certainly not with Bill there. No telling what might come out of the young man's mouth.

"Where's the fire, Lou?" Bill asks as she starts the engine.

"I don't want them to . . . Crosby is always trying to sell me ostrich chicks. He has a ranch and thinks I should quit my job and start raising . . . Move, Bill. Out of the way."

The provost and her husband, both laden with clubs, loom nearer. Lou revs the engine.

"Oh, wow, can't believe . . ." Bill says.

"What?"

"Those shades. I thought they were history."

Before she can hand the sunglasses to him—they're on the dashboard—he's reached in and grabbed them.

"I've been meaning to give them to you, Bill. You left them at Coffee Ridge one day and . . ."

"Dude." He puts them on, and for the first time all afternoon, his face shows some emotion. He's smiling. "Like this is so cool."

"Good, now please move."

As Lou pulls out of the parking lot, the Cobbs are so busy stowing their golf bags they don't notice her go by. She doesn't have to slow down now and thank Crosby for the grand prize that came with the trophy—a gift certificate redeemable for ten kilograms of ostrich chow. And one live chick.

CHAPTER SEVENTEEN

"Knock, knock," Lou says as she lets herself in. "Grady, you here?"

Grady, of course, is at the church's food pantry, where, as Lou well knows, she works every Wednesday from four to six distributing to the needy. Lou waits a moment. It's Wednesday, five on the dot. She has hurried over as soon as she could from WaistWatch.

"Grady?" she calls out again as she heads for the kitchen.

Just as she hoped, Carla is there, alone. Kneading bread, the cook blows a silvery bang out of her eyes. "Hey, Louie."

"The trophy. I thought Grady should have it. For a while."

"She's not here. Just leave it there on the sofa."

Lou sets it down on the horsehair. Then picks it up again. "Rye?"

"Fourteen grain."

Lou admires the trim, muscled arms. Carla looks up, smiles pleasantly.

"They should've put our names on this thing," Lou says, setting the trophy down on the counter. "Sort of tacky not to. By the way, I've got the gift certificate, too. It's in the cup."

"Huh?"

"For the baby ostrich. I thought Grady might like to go and re-deem it herself. Crosby just called me at work and said the chick was still an egg. I told him I didn't have time to hatch it myself so he said fine, send Grady."

The cook slaps flour off her jeans. Poured into them, that's how good Carla looks, like an instructor at WaistWatch. "The grand prize is an egg?"

"You've got to get Grady to swear she won't turn it into an omelette or something. You know how impatient she is. I'd rather not accept the prize at all if she eats it."

"Yeast, where are you?" Carla twirls a spice rack, peers under a sifter. "Come to mama."

"Crosby will give you all sorts of instructions. What centigrade to keep it at and a hot line number . . ." Lou spots the packet of yeast and tosses it over to her. "This is for the bake sale, right? The Arts Council? Can I give you a hand? I'm on the Council, you know."

A nonelectric iron-toothed grinder makes so much noise that Lou has to repeat her offer. Carla then hands Lou the sifter.

"Louie," Carla says a few minutes later as Lou rinses out a mix-ing bowl. From the prewar oven comes the most heavenly aroma. "That husband of yours. What has he done with Mrs. Ompala?"

Lou wrings the sponge. When she confronted Don after the tournament yesterday, he said he was planning to tell her all along—but only if she promised not to say anything to Carla or Bill. Or Grady and Alpha. Don had taken Mrs. Ompala to the Far Plains ranch on the other side of Liberty. This is where Crosby Cobb raises ostriches. And keeps a menagerie—a giraffe, three ze-bras, a small herd of wildebeest, and several Thomson's gazelles. Crosby is letting Mrs. Ompala stay there rent-free in exchange for her services. She helps feed the giraffe and is designing a label for the ostrich meat.

"Oh, she's fine, Carla."

"She's with you, huh? You got all that room."

"There's room, all right. Much more than I need. So it was the right cook, Don told me, the Kikuyu. Mrs. Ompala did give her child to Alpha's mother on that coffee plantation. But that girl was

Alpha's stepsister, much younger. Well, so much for those people searches on the Net. That's how Mrs. O. tracked Alpha down. I have yet to see a computer really help anyone . . . What? You said a cup, right?"

Lou holds the cup of rye over the rinsed bowl. Still staring curiously at her, Carla says, "Has he ever abused you? Physically?"

"Who?"

"Is that why you're separated?"

Lou slams the measuring cup down. "We're not separated. Don is simply . . . I really resent— No man is more gentle and considerate than my husband."

"Grant was thinking of suing him for assault and battery. She was talking to City Hall about it, a superintendent there."

"Pickens is no lawyer."

"Really? Thought he was."

"He's a nut, that's what he is." Lou wrings the sponge again, hard. Moonlighting indeed. And was it really true the man couldn't have seen through the skylight? Why did he move away then, when Mrs. Tudie waved at him? "He was the one stirring up that librarian, making Don seem like some sort of monster."

"Why would Pickens do that?"

"The man was trying to get *Mrs.* Van Buren back in Don's parents' house so he could have an affair with her. Adultery. That's what it all boils down to. Pickens can't have his way with her when she's living with her mother." Now that Lou's finally said it out loud, it doesn't seem so much like conjecture. Nevertheless, she feels slightly ashamed. She's managed to keep all this to herself until now.

Carla gnaws on a strand of gray hair while she amends a recipe on her WordPad. "Who's Mrs. Van Buren? Oh, Burma, Grant's friend, right? The one who married the millionaire?"

"Yes. And I don't think any of this is really her fault. Mrs. Van Buren has been trying, in her own way. But that superintendent . . ."

"In any case, I talked Grant out of suing you guys. Thought you had enough trouble as it was."

Lou tosses the sponge aside. "Look, Carla, I appreciate that. I really do. You're right about Don. He's going through the most awful time. He's still out of a job, and his parents have just died, both of them, and we've got that awful mortgage on Brougham Gardens."

"And that's why you came here, Lou, right? You want me to lay off."

Lou adds millet to the rye. "I don't know what you're talking about."

"Go easy on your friend Rowena."

"She's Grady's friend, really, not mine. I mean I know her, but . . ."

"And you're up for a job at St. Jude."

"The provost doesn't decide that. It's the music faculty."

Carla smiles. "This provost could slide you in easy, Lou. Alpha told me all Rowena has to do is give you the nod and you're in."

"The music faculty chooses, Carla. She just says yes or no to their choice."

"In theory. But in fact, Rowena decides everything in that school. The president himself is scared to death of her."

Lou sponges up oil from the counter. "If you people were really honest, you wouldn't be going after her. You'd be going after Dr. Whitney. *He's* the one who doesn't support affirmative action. Rowena does. For heaven's sake, that's the very reason she hired him. But I know why you and Bill leave him alone."

"Hey, Louie, Rowena should have appointed that Filipina from Stanford, plain and simple. That's who should be dean now. Furthermore, this year alone, she's appointed three department heads, all of whom are male. And the male-female ratio regarding tenure is appalling." Carla wraps a strand of lush gray hair around a thermometer. "I simply can't stand it anymore. It was enough at Yale. But then to come down here and see the same thing . . . No, sir. This gal has had it up to here."

Lou takes the thermometer from beneath Carla's nose and rinses the dough off. "In case you haven't noticed, Carla, I happen to be a woman, too. And you're making sure I never get a decent job at St. Jude."

"Come on, Louie. Be real. Alpha told me you're making more

at WaistWatch than that assistant professor gig would pay. If it's really the mortgage you're concerned about, then Alpha says . . ."

"Yes, Alpha. She's behind all this, I know. She still hasn't forgiven me for firing her."

Carla frowns. "Don't be silly."

"Why won't she speak to me, then? Why does she look down her nose at me? I'm the least racist person I've ever met. Just because my mother's line goes back to Jefferson Davis, can I help that? The Jewish part should cancel that out."

"You're Jewish?"

"Sure. My mother was descended from a Trotsky."

"But Trotsky, that name isn't . . . I mean Trotsky's *real* name was Bronstein. He used 'Trotsky' on a forged passport. It was the name of his jailer and—"

"Oh, for heaven's sake, Carla, my mother's family has nothing to do with *that* Trotsky. They weren't Communists, dear."

Carla sweeps a silken gray strand over her bare shoulder. Such lovely olive skin, smooth as a girl's. "It's that house, right, Louie? You still can't get over Coffee Ridge."

"I'm happy for Alpha. I'm really happy she's been recompensed for all the years she worked for zilch. It's Don who can't . . . I mean, if he had a job, he could see it better. I've been doing my best, I swear, to get him to come back home where he belongs. But he's sort of obsessed, thinks his mother was demented when she wrote the will." Lou's chest aches with each breath. But the heartburn is tolerable if she doesn't get too excited. Kneading, she finds, calms her down. She does this for a few quiet moments while Carla edits her recipes.

"Check the oven, Louie. Quick."

The cast-iron door squeaks open. Lou peers in dutifully, not quite sure what she's supposed to be checking. And she's not sure, either, about this *Louie* business. No one's ever called her that before. "Looks fine."

The phone rings. Lou, who isn't closer, goes over and picks up. It's Fred, Grady's daughter, calling from Joppa. She wants to know if her notes on Hittite phalli are in her top dresser drawer. She thinks she left them there, and would Lou mind FedEx-ing them to her? And by the way, could she also send three boxes of Whitman's Samplers? The crew on the dig really seems to like them.

"Who was that?" Carla asks after Lou hangs up.

Lou explains. Then back at the sink, as she scrubs a blackened pan with steel wool, she asks, "You and Grady. What's going on?"

"Did Bill say anything?"

"No, it's me . . . I know it's none of my business but . . ." She turns from the sink, hands dripping. "It's fine with me, Carla—if you are. I don't have a problem with it." Lou hates the tone she's adopted now—so patronizing. A prim spinster's.

"Relax, Louie. Grady's not my type. Little Miss Whitebread, no thank you."

"She seems to like you. A lot."

"Miss Sigma Chi is not gay."

"I've never seen her so . . . lively. The shower yesterday."

Carla shrugs. "She's hung up on men, Louie. Hopeless. Can't cure her now. So what's with the oven! You left the door open."

On the gallery, sipping coffee, Lou watches a thrush below. It's after eight, no time for a bird to be dining. But there it is, wandering in and out of the lamplight, pecking at the few strands of St. Augustine beneath the live oaks. To a cricket, the bird must be more monstrous than a T. rex, cruel, implacable. On two legs, upright, it moves like a dinosaur. Where are its arms, though? Even T. rex had spindly arms.

"Wings."

"Pardon?" Carla is stretched out on a chaise longue beside her. They've eaten half a loaf of fourteen grain for supper. For some reason, it was the best meal Lou can remember. Just the plain bread, dipped in olive oil. No cheese. No wine. But she savored every bite. Carla must be some sort of genius with bread.

"Wings—that's their arms." And Lou explains about the thrush below.

"Maybe God sees dinosaurs as we see birds," Carla says.

"They're pretty much the same thing, too. Some scientists think birds descended from . . ."

"Why aren't dinosaurs in Genesis? I mean, if this really is the actual word of God, why is all that left out?"

"I swear, Lou. You sound like a Fundamentalist."

"And they're all wiped out. All the dinosaurs, just like that. What was the point? Millions of years of evolution and . . . poof. An asteroid falls on them. It's as awful as that Noah's ark business. God destroying his own creation. I've never understood why it's all right for him to get furious and destroy almost everything."

"God isn't man, Louie. That's your mistake. He can't be judged by us."

"But if he clearly breaks universal moral laws, the conscience that he instilled in us in the first place? To drown almost all of creation, innocent babies, animals, then to massacre innocent Egyptians. Those firstborn hadn't done anything wrong."

"Louie, Louie—don't you see? It's all about the underdog. What makes the Torah so great, it's showing that God is on the side of the underdog. All those rich fat cats, the sleek pharaohs, they're shown that their power, their wealth, is nothing. And besides, Jews always respected other races. Job himself wasn't a Jew. Neither was Abraham."

They've been talking this way since the bread came piping hot from the oven. Lou can't seem to get enough. She's been so hungry, malnourished by Lynda at WaistWatch, her junk-food answers. Grady, who returned from the church pantry with a bucket of Popeye's, has been driven from the field. She's upstairs in her room, munching extra-spicy wings in peace.

"Carla," Lou says as Hyla sing from a puddle under the eaves, "did you ever think that Mrs. Ompala might be some sort of . . . saint? I always had the feeling she was in touch with . . . Like other dimensions."

From the dark—Carla's just switched off the gallery light—comes: "Get a grip, Louie."

"Well, how do we know for sure?"

"Believe me, I know. I've spent hours and hours with her. It's impossible to really pin her down on anything. One minute she's talking about Mombasa, then she's going on about the farm outside Nairobi, the coffee plantation. I've really begun to wonder if she's not confusing herself with something she's read. Like Dinesen."

"Well, more than one woman in the world has lived on a coffee plantation outside Nairobi. And besides, Dinesen never did research at Oxford—all that stuff."

"Right, all that bishop bullshit, Lady Fitzhoward. Straight out of Waugh—or Wodehouse, maybe. I'm not saying she's consciously lying. It's just that a lot of what she's read has gotten mixed up with . . ."

"But why is it so impossible that her uncle was a bishop? Or her aunt a Lady? And besides, I looked up Evesham, where the swineherd saw the Virgin. It's all there, you know. She didn't make that up."

"She didn't make up Mississippi either, Louie."

The darkness, more soothing than her usual Gibsons, seems what Lou has always longed for—without quite knowing it. "My life would sound just as suspicious, as if I were making it up as I went along . . ."

Her eyes still adjusting, Lou cannot define any fixed shape for this woman beside her. But a delectable scent is there—cedar, nutmeg, some spice Lou can't quite decipher.

"My father, you know, he used to live out there."

Where?

Was that a *where?* Or did she just imagine the faint encouragement?

"The toolshed. He had nowhere else to go. Grady's father took him in. He was a refugee from the Nazis. But the INS never believed he was in any real danger. Because he was Catholic, studying to be a priest. They tried to deport him. It was Grady's father—Judge Morgen. Hid him here. Could've got in trouble himself for sheltering an illegal alien if he weren't so . . . Knew how to grease the right palms. Got my father a shoe shop even though he wasn't supposed to work here."

Really?

"Mom told me things my father never knew, how Judge Morgen got an INS agent jailed, planted morphine in the guy's glove compartment, Mrs. Morgen's sleeping pills. That's how my father was left in peace."

Cicadas, buried fourteen years, have sprung from the ground to compete with the tree frogs.

"My mother was very practical, down-to-earth. If it weren't for her, we probably wouldn't have survived. Before she married my Dad, Carla, she was . . ."

What? Go on.

"His secretary, Judge Morgen's. It was Judge Morgen who hooked her up with my father. Thought my father needed someone like her—tough, practical."

Are you saying . . . ?

"What? No, no, of course not. There was never anything between them."

Your mother and Judge Morgen?

"No. She wasn't his type. Floozies, blond floozies, that's what he liked. My mom, tough as nails. She'd never allow any . . ."

"Any what?"

Lou starts. "Carla?" The voice is suddenly so strange, not right at all.

Craning her neck, she sees someone standing behind the empty chaise longue.

"Where's Carla? I thought . . ."

The porch light flicks on. "The ladies'," Bill says.

"Oh. Well, better head 'em on up, move 'em on out." Lou's right foot is asleep, though. She can't get up quite yet.

"Huh?" Bill perches on the edge of the chaise longue, where Carla isn't. White socks he has on, with some sort of plastic sandal. It would never do in Lou's day, this getup. Don once came to school with white socks and sandals. Lou nearly died. She made him go home and change.

"Got to get on home," Lou explicates.

"So what's a floozie?"

"You really got into Yale, Bill? I sometimes find it hard to believe."

Carla has the guest bathroom occupied, so Lou hurries to the servants' washroom right off the kitchen. She won't be able to make it home without relieving herself first. After pulling the chain to flush, she remembers that she hasn't taken her estrogen today. It's in her handbag. And her handbag is out on the gallery. She left the butler in such a hurry that she forgot to bring it along.

"No, I don't think you're some sort of flake," she replies to Bill's direct question after scrounging around in the dark for the handbag. Bill has turned off the light on the gallery, and she can't find the switch.

"That's what your husband called me."

Lou takes a deep breath. It's hard enough explaining her own words and actions sometimes, but to have to translate her husband's, as well . . . "Don sometimes gets excited, Bill. He doesn't really mean what he says. Underneath it all, you won't find a more decent, sensitive human being."

"He jumped all over me for doing an e-mail alert about Dr. Cobb."

"What alert?"

"A Log Cabin alert."

"Good heavens, don't tell me you're a Republican."

"Got a problem with it?"

"I sure do, Bill. When my husband refused to vote for McGovern, I wouldn't speak to him for an entire week."

"McGovern?"

"You know, the guy who ran against Taft."

Bill dangles a sandal by one toe. "But like you voted for Pickens, didn't you? He's a Republican."

"Only because I was told that pervert didn't have an ice cube's chance in . . ."

"Queer. The word is queer, Mrs. Jones."

"I don't mean queer, gay, whatever. I mean Pickens climbs up on people's roofs and spies on them. He was spying on me just the other night, peering down through our skylight."

Bill turns his head now. In fact, he's even raised his shades for a better view of her. "You're shitting me."

"I swear. I had this funny feeling I was being watched. I kept on telling myself to stop thinking that, it was crazy. But then—I was doing the dishes, see, or something like that, you know—and I happened to glance up at the skylight and there he was. Peering right down at me."

"Shut up."

"Scout's honor." She holds up two fingers. "Bill, it's really true. Politicians down here in Louisiana, you have no idea how far-out they can be."

"But why was he . . . ? What was he doing up there?"

Lou touches his knee lightly. "Moonlighting. He wants to buy a Miata, so he's working with the tax assessor, Mrs. Tudie. She owns the company—AAA SecureCare—and sort of had to hire him, even though she loathes him, because he's family."

"Wait, hold on a sec." Now he's sitting up. "That's the company that stole those red A's?"

Lou will have to detour around this question. When three red A's appeared on SecureCare's sign, Mrs. Melvin Tudie suffered considerable embarrassment. In the *Herald*, she expressed her outrage that she would be accused of stealing A's for her company's sign, which had been getting by with only a single black A for the past twelve years. If this had been the end of the story, Lou could have died happy, thankful that there was some justice in the world. Unfortunately, after she read the front-page story aloud to Don, he casually mentioned that it had worked. He had borrowed the A's from the Cineplex and put them up on Mrs. Tudie's sign. As revenge. She's on the zoning board that ruined Brougham Gardens with commercial development. It was why Don couldn't unload the house there for a fair price.

"Anyway, I was finishing the dishes and the next thing I know, there's Superintendent Pickens on the roof peering down at us— *me.*"

"You think Pickens stole those A's, Lou?"

She opens her purse and fishes for her keys. "Walk me to my

car, Bill. I don't have good night vision and might stumble on one of those roots."

He gets up and with a slight bow, takes her arm. "So it *was* Pickens."

The first step off the gallery is so far down that she must grab his bony shoulder to steady herself. "I never said that, Bill. Now take it easy, not so fast."

CHAPTER EIGHTEEN

In the midst of filling up her cart at the Jitney Jungle, Lou feels dizzy, a little faint. A few catfish nuggets might help her get through her list. Just a snack, something to absorb the acid in the diet pills she had just taken. After ordering from the deli counter, Lou glances over at the alcove to see if one of the picnic tables is free. At first she doesn't recognize her. But as she gets closer, nuggets in hand, Lou realizes it's Maigrite, sitting alone on a bench, her face drawn, ashen. Something is wrong, Lou can sense. She prays quickly that Maigrite hasn't just been to the doctor, that she has no news.

"Hon," Lou says as she sits down at the table, "is everything all right?"

Hunched over her collards, Maigrite forks the bacon fat from one side of the plate to the other. It's plain she hasn't eaten a thing.

"Dear, how about some coffee?" Lou persists. "Let me get you a nice cup of coffee."

Maigrite raises her eyes. She looks blankly at Lou, as if she doesn't recognize her. Lou's so used to seeing her in the office's dim, flattering light, the faint rose. Here the harsh fluorescent tubes would make even the halest construction worker seem a little sickly. Much less Maigrite, who's positively shivering in her angora.

"He's leaving me." Maigrite reaches out and takes Lou's chapped hand. "The superintendent's leaving me."

"Dear heart, are you sure?"

"He's moving out today. Lou, he's going to live with his brother down on Sweetgum."

"I didn't know he had a brother."

Magnified by tears that won't fall, Maigrite's eyes seem as large and wondrous as a child's. "It's a half brother, F.X. I wouldn't ever let him in my house, Lou. He's a horrible man. An ex-con that runs that restaurant over on North Gladiola."

"Oh, my. And they serve such wonderful angel-hair."

"What?"

"It is overpriced, though," Lou reassures her with a squeeze to the bony hand. "How they stay in business, I'll never know. Hardly anyone there when I go. Not that I eat there a lot. It's criminal, what they charge for . . ."

"Girl, would you please stop blathering about that place." Maigrite's annoyance is such a relief to Lou. More like her old self.

"Keep in mind, hon, when men get his age, they all go a little nuts. Don't worry, Mr. Pickens is going to fly right back to his cage."

"His *cage*?"

"Well, Maigrite, that's what men think after a while. They begin to feel marriage is like a cage. You got to let them flap free for a while, get buzzed by a few hawks, see how hard it is to find those worms, then they'll be homing back in, glad to, you know . . ."

"Worms? Hawks?" Maigrite says while a uniformed maintenance man at the other table talks on his cell phone. "For heaven's sake, Louise. My husband has left me for another woman and you go on about . . ."

"Now, Maigrite, let's not jump to any conclusions."

"You're the one who's been warning me about that woman. I just didn't want to believe she was capable of such . . ."

"I'm here at the Jitney Jungle now," the maintenance man says in a loud voice, as if to someone hard of hearing. "I'm having my lunch now. Yes, that's what I'm doing, Papa. I'm sitting right here having my lunch. I come get you jest as soon as I done finished this lunch. I'm having my lunch now, hear?"

"Maigrite, can't we . . ."

"Yes, I know it's past two. That's when I have my lunch, Papa. I'm having my lunch now. No, it's not Friday. This here's Saturday. Don't you tell me it's Friday, Papa, when you know good and well it's Saturday."

"Maigrite, let's go somewhere else, please. I can't think here. Let me buy you a nice lunch at . . ." The maintenance man's voice makes it hard for Lou to focus. Thanks to him, she strayed into hawks and worms earlier. "Just come."

"My greens."

"They're cold, Maigrite. I'll get you some nice hot greens. Without that horrible bacon grease that you know Brother Moodie wouldn't approve of."

"Oh, to hell with Brother Moodie."

"Come along, dear."

They decide to leave Maigrite's car in the Jitney Jungle parking lot. Her heater isn't working, and there's a nip in the air. Lou first heads for the Bengali restaurant she's been meaning to try for so long. It's out by the video poker software plant that, like the Waist-Watch franchise, doesn't have to pay any state taxes. Halfway there, when they're passing Trump's Alligator Farm, Maigrite suddenly stops crying and asks where Lou is fixing to take her. When Lou explains, Maigrite says she is not eating in any restaurant that serves goat.

"Who says they serve goat?" Lou asks in a calmer, more reasonable tone of voice.

"The superintendent. He had to eat there once after he got them the tax break from the city."

"Well, even if they do serve it, it doesn't mean you have to order it."

"Turn around."

"Maigrite."

"I swear I'll jump out of this car if you don't turn around."

There's a rumor that a Ruby Tuesday is opening up by Wal-Mart. Lou reminds Maigrite that this is only a rumor as the BMW heads clear across town. Maigrite, though, insists she saw an ad for it on Channel 237 when she was watching the Christmas parade.

"The Christmas parade? That was back in October, Maigrite. They couldn't have advertised way back then."

"This was a rerun, just last night. Funny how you have this accent, Lou."

Waiting for an inordinately long light at the Tula Springs Industrial Park intersection, Lou asks what she means by that, an accent.

"On TV, you sound like you're from England or Austria or something."

"Australia? That's nonsense."

"I swear. If I closed my eyes, I'd think you weren't from these parts at all."

"Well, Maigrite, when you're on TV, you have to enunciate. And the camera adds five pounds, you know. That's a fact."

As a color commentator for the parade back in October, Lou had been required to trot with a microphone beside the floats and convertibles. The instructions she was getting from the director over her earpiece were almost unintelligible. So she got the president of BancSouth mixed up with the Yam Queen. When she saw the tape that Don had recorded off his VCR, she wept bitter tears. The earpiece made her head seem lopsided. And she dangled so many participles.

"Would you *please* go?" Maigrite urges after seven minutes, when the light finally changes. As usual there isn't any traffic either coming or going to the Park, which has no industry yet—only two hundred acres of tree stumps.

"It's green?"

"Yes, that's what we call green, Louise."

As Lou predicted, Ruby Tuesday is indeed only a rumor. Maigrite rolls down the window and peers hard at the empty lot. "I don't see how they can advertise something that's not even here."

"Dear, I have a feeling they were advertising the one in Missis-sippi. At the mall."

"There you go again. Sounding like Queen Mary."

"You mean Elizabeth the Second."

"No, I mean the Queen Mother."

The BMW pulls into Wholly Mackerel, where a debate ensues. Maigrite doesn't want to go inside. She hates the smell of fish.

"Look, I thought Alpha cooked you some fish once," Lou says as she pulls back onto the highway. "For that fellowship dinner with Brother Moodie. How can you hate the smell of fish?"

"I just do. And please don't mention that woman's name to me."

"Alpha? Why shouldn't I mention her?"

"Because she's the reason the superintendent moved out on me."

"What?"

"Here's a Sonic, Lou. Let's stop here."

Lou is unable to make a left turn soon enough, though. They must drive past.

"Maigrite, explain what you just said. About Alpha."

"Alpha is *her* landlady now. That woman's."

"Burma's?"

Maigrite nods. "The superintendent asked Alpha if she'd rent Burma a room at Coffee Ridge. So now Burma won't be living with her mother anymore. She's moving in next week. I'm just positive that's why the superintendent moved out on me."

Lou ponders this while trying to think of another place to eat. In one sense, she's relieved that Don and Alpha won't be living alone any longer. There was something not quite right about that arrangement. As a matter of fact, there's no way Don will want to stay there now. Not with the woman he himself evicted. How could they possibly get along in the same house? Yes, this is indeed good news.

"Take me home, Lou."

"You have to eat," Lou reminds her boss. "You really are getting far too thin. And by the way, you should give Burma more credit. She's a very honest woman who wouldn't dream of stealing someone's husband. She told me herself that once you're married, that's it."

Maigrite sighs. "Turn."

"But this is Sweetgum."

"Turn, dammit."

Lou swerves, running onto the shoulder. For years, ever since her father died, Lou's managed to avoid this street. Since it's not on the way to anything, this hasn't been hard.

"Stop!" Maigrite grabs Lou's arm, digging in with sculpted magenta nails.

"Here? You sure this is it, hon?"

"Five seventeen. This is the ex-con's all right. There's his car, plain as day. And there's my *mamaw's* dresser, her good loblolly dresser that's got twenty-one drawers."

Not heeding Lou's warnings, Maigrite flings open the car door right in the middle of the street. Before Lou can pull over, her boss is striding through monkey grass and aspidistra. The dresser is halfway in the front door—stuck, apparently.

Behind Lou, a van honks. With her arm out the window, Lou motions for the driver to pass around her. Another honk. The van is baby blue, with "City of Tula S Public Transportation" painted freehand across the hood.

After an impatient tattoo from the van, Lou has no choice now, but pulls into the driveway—not the ex-con's, but the one next door. This is the house where her father died—a stroke, sudden, swift, and final. He was bringing Communion to Mrs. Wedge, who lived alone, barely mobile because of a botched hip replacement. Lou was in bed with Melvin Tudie when Mrs. Wedge phoned, asking Lou to please hurry over, as if she were just next door, not three states away. This was while Lou was getting her Ph.D. in Tallahassee. Melvin had shown up at her doorstep, unannounced. He was married by then. It was brave of him to have come to see her, to ask about the operation, as he called it. The child that never was. They stood in the tiny room littered with Schoenberg scores, measures she had painstakingly copied from *Verklärte Nacht*, monographs, the beans cold on her hotplate, Spam propping up a *Grove's Dictionary*. He held her. For five minutes she found comfort, peace in his arms. That was all it was meant to be. A little reassurance, a private memorial to help them both get on with their lives. But oh, the man, such shoulders, so massive, and he, unlike Don, taller than she, heavier, too, with those cruel Robert Mitchum eyes . . . She realized then how much she had wanted that child. How she and Don could have somehow worked out an arrangement, perhaps. The room where she studied, wrote, graded freshman theory quizzes, and ate Spam was also the room she slept in. Even if it was so little sleep, so little rest. On the battered Salvation Army couch were laid out the revised versions of the first, third, and twenty-third chapters of her dissertation. In her haste to clear a space, three pages of the first found their way into the twenty-third. It would be such an embarrassment later, when the bound volume would be queried by her director at Florida State. And have to be rebound when she hadn't a cent to spare. When it would mean doing without Spam.

"Come help me!" Maigrite calls from the other yard.

Lou gets out of the BMW and crosses through a hedge of sugarcane. After inspecting the dresser, Lou tells her boss it's futile. Even if they could get it out the door, they'd never be able to lug it across the yard. And the scrolled loblolly wouldn't fit in the BMW anyway. Way too big for the trunk.

"If that man thinks he's going to take my *mamaw's* dresser . . ." Maigrite declares. Lou has escorted her back to the car in Mrs. Wedge's driveway, where Maigrite wants to wait for the superintendent or his half brother to show up. But Lou has started the engine. She has no intention of getting embroiled in a domestic altercation. Besides, a young woman has just come out of the neat, compact house at the end of the drive. She stuffs a garbage bag into a bin under the eaves of the carport and then turns and stares in their direction.

"Cut off that engine, Lou. I'm not budging until . . ."

"Maigrite, we can't sit in someone's driveway like this and . . . By the way, I don't think Mary is the Queen Mother. She's actually . . . Oh, hello." The young woman, either pregnant or dumpy, but with the prettiest face, a throwback to the solid innocence of the Fifties, has padded barefoot down the drive to the car. "How is Mrs. Wedge?" Lou finds herself saying to the girl. Yes, just a girl, really. Barely grown up.

"Who?"

"The lady who used to live here. Is she still alive?"

The young woman shrugs.

"Well, if she is, please give her my regards." Lou smiles pleasantly as she puts the car in reverse. The girl shrugs again and kicks a pinecone off the drive.

"My car! That man has taken my car, too!"

Lou has driven Maigrite back to her own house, where Lou plans to make her a nice bowl of chicken soup with a good dollop of schmaltz.

"He's taking everything. How will I get to work without my car?"

"Don't worry, dear. I'll come by and get you. It's not that much out of my way." As Lou makes this promise, she remembers: they've left Maigrite's car in the parking lot at Jitney Jungle.

"See?" Lou says after reminding her boss. "He's not taking everything. I tell you, Maigrite, Mr. Pickens will be back. I guarantee."

"Now what? This isn't the way."

"I know." But Lou must stop by her house before they return to Jitney Jungle. She has a lot of frozen food in the backseat, and she must get it into her freezer before it thaws.

CHAPTER NINETEEN

Having referred thirty-nine friends and acquaintances to WaistWatch during the past fiscal year, Lou is awarded a plaque that will grace the wall of the aerobics workout room. It was supposed to be hung during the presentation ceremony that afternoon, but the fiberboard gave way. Lou explained to Maigrite, who had put up the hook for the plaque, that a stud should have been found to anchor the hook. You can't just pound things straight into fiberboard.

"Some people have no idea there are certain physical laws that can't be ignored," Lou comments to Don that evening at Coffee Ridge. She's still wearing the Gaultier ensemble he had given her for their anniversary, two days ago. The cut seems a little too daring for a fifty-four-year-old, and Lou almost hadn't had the nerve to wear it to the ceremony with the staff. But Lynda knew right away what she had on. *"Gaultier!"* she cried out with a clap of her hands. "Oh, Lou. Jean Paul Gaultier! It's the most stunning . . ."

"I feel like an idiot, Lynda. Purple and khaki, orange, I don't get it."

"Priceless."

Unfortunately, not. Someone had forgotten to remove the sales slip from the gift box. Lou's head reeled when she saw what Don had spent. If only Lynda were her size, Lou would have offered it to her, at a nice discount. As it was, she would have to see if somehow, some way, the skirt, fisherman's net vest, and cape could be returned.

"That's it?" Don says, handing her another Gibson. "A plaque? No bonus, no raise?"

It's made exactly right, the drink. No one, not even she herself, can make a Gibson like Don. "I'm sure I'll be getting a raise sometime. This is just a little recognition along the way. *L'chaim*, my love!"

They clink glasses. Lou is still feeling a glow—not from the first Gibson, but from the presentation. Every member of the staff, from Tifawni in hair sculpting to Brother Moodie himself, gave a short tribute to Lou. Not only that, each and every one hugged her—Maigrite included. Lou felt such love for these people. It was a shame that Don didn't appreciate them. He could be pretty narrow-minded for an Episcopalian.

"Dr. Jones!" comes a faraway cry.

Lou, who thought they were alone in the house, sets her drink down beside a pink cow whose belly doles out sugar cubes. "I thought Alpha was at school, Don."

"She is. They've got a meeting with a state legislator about Rowena."

"Then you mean that's . . . ?"

"Now look, Lou. Before you get all steamed, she's only here on a temporary basis."

"But you told me she wasn't coming here at all. You said Maigrite had it all wrong. Didn't know what the hell she was talking about—I quote."

With a napkin, Don wipes egg yolk off a Contented Cow saltshaker. "Look, I did my best to convince Alpha it wasn't a good idea to have a boarder. Honest, babe. I talked till I was blue in the face. But she wouldn't budge. She said she'd already promised Pickens."

"Dr. Jones!"

"Stay put, Don. *I'll* see what she wants."

Lou swerves briskly through the kitchen door and pauses a

moment in the living room, where she has an odd feeling. Yes, it is different. Maybelle's portrait of a Guernsey, a head with huge, yearning eyes, has been replaced by a matador on black velvet.

In the hallway Lou wanders from one end to the other, opening all the wrong doors—Don's bedroom, a bathroom, Alpha's bedroom—until finally . . .

"Oh, Dr. Jones," Mrs. Van Buren says, her back to Lou. The woman is in a drab chenille robe with matching polish on her toenails. "Help me, will you? This thing is stuck. I've been yanking on it, just a-yanking and a-yanking and . . . Lou!"

"Yes, dear, it's me. What seems to be the problem?"

Mrs. Van Buren gives the dresser a plump kick. "This drawer is stuck. I can't get to my panties. Do you have any lard, Lou? Doesn't have to be Crisco, though that actually works best for when you get stuck, you know."

Lou explains to Mrs. Van Buren that she's not in the habit of carrying lard around with her. Whether Alpha has some in the kitchen is another story. It's her house, after all.

On her way out, Lou tries to make her collision with Mrs. Van Buren's Louis Vuitton steamer trunk somehow the trunk's fault. Shameless in her modest frayed robe, something a granny might wear with impunity if the granny had the common decency not to mention she wasn't wearing any panties, Mrs. Van Buren apologizes for the trunk and asks if Lou might want a cup of black coffee. Lou, who had drunk three flutes of sherbert punch at the ceremony before being told it was laced with chartreuse—Brother Moodie allows the inner staff a taste of spirits on special occasions—continues down the hall without bothering to reply.

Back in the kitchen, Lou asks Don what is meant by that dresser.

"What dresser?"

"That dresser in Mrs. Van Buren's room. Do you realize it belongs to *mamaw*?"

"*Mamaw*?"

"Maigrite's grandmother. Mr. Pickens stole that priceless antique from Maigritte when he moved out last week."

"Well, I hope you don't expect *me* to take it back. Nearly killed me and Pickens, moving it in here. Had to take the door off Burma's bedroom."

"There's only one thing to do, Don. You're going to have to pack up. Move on back home."

He takes a bite of the egg whites Benedict he had fixed for her supper. "But the house, Lou."

"My dear child, you might as well face facts. It's Alpha's. Plain and simple. There's no way you can prove your mother was nuts."

"What about all these cows, that portrait she painted of her best friend?"

Lou ponders this a moment. "Where is that painting anyway? Didn't it used to hang over the sofa?"

"I put it in my bedroom. Burma wanted something to remind her of home, so she hung up that toreador."

They both gaze in the direction of the living room, as if the phosphorescent velvet were awful enough to radiate through a closed door.

"All I've heard, Don, is how she can't stand living at home with her mother. Now you're telling me she wants to be reminded of it? Let her move back, then. She'll be reminded plenty."

"Aren't you being a little harsh?"

She takes his fork away from him and savors the last bite of his Benedict. This, too, is perfection. So good that she accepts his offer for another, one for the road.

"Lou?" he says, refreshing the hollandaise sauce with a few drops of Cointreau, "I always thought you liked Burma. You were always telling me to take it easy, don't worry about collecting the back rent from her. Now why are you suddenly being so hard on her?"

"Would you stop with the hard and the harsh? You're the one told me I should always refer to her as 'Mrs. Van Buren.'"

"Well, things are different now, babe. She's really not such a bad egg after all."

"Is that a fact? The woman's rooked us out of three months'

rent, she nearly got you sued for assaulting a lesbian, and she's carrying on with a married man who happens to be my boss's husband . . . Don't make faces, Don. I'm just stating facts."

The poacher steams merrily as he shakes his head. "There's nothing going on between Burma and Pickens. They're just friends, Lou. Can't a man and woman be friends in this day and age?"

"Not when the man moves out on his wife. That's not the time to start making friends with a woman."

"Maigrite is pretty rough on him. She bosses him something awful, Burma says. Won't let him see his brother. Won't let him drink or smoke. Makes him go to church twice on Sundays."

"Toast is burning."

He dashes to the island and rescues a slice of Carla's homemade rye. After buttering it, Lou is in heaven. She can't believe how good everything tastes this evening.

"So what's wrong with making someone toe the line?" Lou says after wiping up the last drop of sauce with the rye. "You ask me, Pickens could use church twice a day, every day."

Though everything is actually contrary, wrong, not the way she would want it, though Lou is unhappy that Mrs. Van Buren is lurking in the back bedroom, either innocent or not innocent of being corrupted by a married man, Lou still hasn't shaken off the wonderful sense of well-being that flooded her at the ceremony. Those hugs. Brother Moodie's little pinch, too, making her screech as Lynda was admiring her Gaultier. Just like a naughty boy, a great big bad boy. Everyone laughed at her screech, all those gorgeous creatures, who did a little screeching themselves as the punch bowl emptied. It was such delightful fun, like being a cheerleader again, head cheerleader. So alive Lou feels, so full of a strange, perplexing, totally unmerited, unreasonable joy that she can't help giving Don a little pinch.

"Lou!" he says, but keeps right on doing the dishes, his back to her.

"What? I didn't do nothing."

"You keep that up and . . ."

"And what?"

"You're going to find yourself in a peck of trouble."

"Trouble's my middle name. Come on. Take me back home, Donnie. Now."

"I've got to finish these dishes."

She's peeled off his apron, Alpha's actually. The one Maybelle hand-stitched for her, bordered with Jerseys.

"Oh, Don, I think I might be, you know, sort of in love with you."

"Quite the romantic, aren't we?"

"Come home, Donnie Boy. Home to Mommy."

"The dishes . . . can't leave them like this. If Alpha came back and saw . . ."

Lou tugs him toward the back door. "Come on, big ole mean man, come home and take care of Mommy. No, not the island. I'm not . . ."

"Lou, hon?" comes Mrs. Van Buren's sweet voice from the other side of the door to the dining room. As it swings open, Don, with a sure, practiced hand, manages to stuff himself back in his jeans and zip up, all in one fluid motion.

"Did you find any lard yet?" Mrs. Van Buren says. She's shed the drab robe and now has on an Ann Taylor ensemble selected by Lynda for the TotalPackageMakeover. "I still can't get that blame drawer open. How am I supposed to go out tonight if I don't get that drawer open?"

"You're going out?" Lou says as Mrs. Van Buren roots through the cabinets.

"Carla and me want to try out that new Cineplex."

"The cook?" Lou says, whisking Don's cowboy belt up off the floor. She hands the thick leather to him while Mrs. Van Buren fusses with the cabinets. "Grady Morgen's cook?"

"Yeah, we're going to this remake of *Thelma and Louise*."

"How nice. What's it called?"

"*Thelma and Louise*." With a grunt Mrs. Van Buren lifts a can of AOL lard from the top shelf.

"What's that for?" Don says, flicking the can with his washrag. "You're not planning to start cooking now, Burma, are you? I'm just about through cleaning up."

"My panties, Dr. Jones. It's for my panties."

"Huh?"

"Never mind, Don," Lou says, picking up the lard. "I'll take care of this myself. Come, Burma. Let's see what a little grease will do."

CHAPTER TWENTY

After the 7:10 A.M. aerobics class is over, Lou reshelves Brother Moodie's CD, *Rappin' Sons of Thunder,* and mists the room with a potpourri spray. There's just enough time before the next class to hang her plaque. She wants to put it over the hole left by Maigrite's ineptness the day before, but her stud-finder does not beep in that area. In fact, she can't seem to find a single stud in the entire room.

"How in the world did Brother Moodie manage to hang all those pictures of himself in there?" she complains a few minutes later to Maigrite. "I don't see how they stay up."

"Is he going to bring that dresser back today, Lou?"

"Who? Don? Honey, I've already told you, he's got to watch his back."

Maigrite has been bringing up the dresser every two minutes—as if it were Lou's responsibility. Maigrite happened to have left out some relevant information when she had her fit about the dresser over on Sweetgum. She never told Lou that Mr. Pickens had *bought* the dresser from Maigrite's grandmother. Paid the old lady $3,000 for it, cash, at Maigrite's insistence. Is it any wonder that Mr. Pickens might think it belonged to him now? This was what Burma had told Lou last night when Lou was in her bedroom with the lard, which did no good whatsoever. In fact, when Lou woke up this morning in Burma's bed with a terrible hangover, the worst she's ever had in her entire life, the first thought that crossed her mind was roaches. All that lard was bound to attract them. In her Gaultier—for some reason, she had fallen asleep fully dressed—she scrubbed the lard off the dresser drawer, even before getting herself a nice steaming cup of black coffee.

"I've a good mind to call the police," Maigrite grumbles.

"Dear, your husband *is* the police."

Still without a police force, Tula Springs relies upon private enterprise to keep the town law-abiding. Of the three private firms that patrol the streets, Mrs. Melvin Tudie's is the largest and most aggressive.

"It's not fair, Lou. It's just not fair."

With tears in her own eyes, Lou takes her boss's frail hands and gives them a good squeeze. She can't stand seeing the poor woman in such distress.

"We'll see this through, Maigrite. I guarantee you're going to get Mr. Pickens back home."

"Who wants that two-timing old . . ."

"Now, let's not talk ugly."

"She can have him. See what I care."

"Honey, you're beginning to sound just like the fox and the . . ." A migraine-like pain nearly blinds Lou for a moment. And it sears into her chest, as well. "You know."

"What?"

"Those things he can't reach."

"Go away, Louise. I can't take any of your crazy talk this morning." She flaps a veined hand, as if shooing away a smelly pet.

Back at the reception desk, dosing herself with take-out latte, Lou wonders if Maigrite has ever heard of Aesop. Cultural illiteracy is so rampant nowadays that it's becoming a chore for an educated person to converse at all. After searching in her drawer, Lou washes down four herbal diet pills with her latte. Then some estrogen.

A pleasant tingling in her loins makes Lou wonder about combining ephedra with estrogen. But when the tingling gets worse, she remembers.

"It's for you," Maigrite says before Lou can pick up the receiver.

"Oh."

"I'll transfer it. But in the future, I'd appreciate not having to reroute your personal calls. From your *dear* friends."

Not sure what to make of this, Lou vaguely apologizes as a second tingle heralds the transfer. "Hello?"

"Lou, are you all right, hon? I've been so worried."

It's Burma, Mrs. Van Buren. Lou says she's fine and please, please don't ever call her at work again. Especially on the wrong extension.

"She didn't have any right to sound so snooty to me," Mrs. Van Buren says. "This is a free country. I'm not doing anything wrong."

"Yes, dear, I know you're not doing anything wrong. And you know you're not doing a thing wrong. But Maigrite . . ."

"I'm the one told him he ought to stay with her. I'm the one got mad at Mr. Pickens for moving out to his brother's."

"Yes, of course. But Maigrite is having a hard time believing this, dear. You've got to watch your P's and Q's."

"Lou, please, don't let's talk about her. I just wanted to tell you not to worry about my mattress. Most of the vomit didn't seep through. I laundered the mattress cover with the sheets and it's practically good as new."

"Look, I promised you at breakfast, hon. A new Beautyrest."

"Lou, you really shouldn't drink so much."

"It wasn't that. It was that hollandaise Don made. I have a very delicate system. Lactose intolerant. Don admitted he forgot and put butter in it."

"Oh. But what about all those Gibsons you had?"

"What Gibsons?"

"When you and Carla started playing Hearts."

"Hearts?"

"After we got back home from *Thelma and Louise*."

Until this moment, Lou was under the impression this card game, where she and Carla were having so much fun with Don, was only an idle daydream. How he roared when he caught them cheating . . .

"You know Don doesn't like to drink alone, Burma. Now I've got to hang up. We're not allowed personal calls at work."

The phone back in its cradle, Lou sits innocently for a moment or two, waiting for Maigrite to say something. But a full ten minutes go by, fifteen, without a word from her boss. Finally, Lou can't take it anymore.

"Look, Maigrite," Lou says after crossing to the module on the other side of the room. "I know what you must be thinking. But whatever it is, stop. Listen to me."

A stony look, an ashen face give Lou pause. But she forges ahead. "You ought to be thanking me, Maigrite."

"For what? Being two-faced? Helping that woman steal my husband and my *mamaw's* priceless dresser that the Choctaws tried to ruin with their varnish?"

"The Choctaws? Look, that dresser is warped so bad you can't open any of the drawers. And as for that husband of yours . . ."

"Don't you dare open your mouth against the superintendent." The fire in Maigrite's eyes, this fierce loyalty, gives Lou hope.

"All I'm saying, Maigrite, is that Mrs. Van Buren won't have him. She won't even let him set foot in the house now. I made her promise me last night."

"Tell me another one, Mother Goose."

Despite this sarcasm, Maigrite looks up from her virtual trash bin with hope skulking in her weary, sunken eyes.

"I'm going to make sure that that woman keeps her hands off Mr. Pickens. He's not setting foot in Coffee Ridge, not if I have anything to do with it. And if you want that dresser back, I'll . . . Well, maybe we can rent a U-Haul and . . . Burma—Mrs. Van Buren—has a friend who works for U-Haul. We could maybe get a deal."

Maigrite's gaze is back on the screen. *Are you sure you want to send totalpackgmkovrVB64x0Z to the trash bin?* Lou reads over her shoulder.

"And you want to know something else, Maigrite? I'm determined to get that money out of her—for the makeover she's never paid for. Out of her husband, I mean. Mrs. Van Buren has been exploited long enough. That husband of hers is going to give her a decent income or I'll have the law on him."

No, Maigrite clicks. "He's in a wheelchair, Lou."

"A golf cart. And for heaven's sake, he's a multimillionaire, while Burma's out buying groceries with food stamps."

"Did you really throw up in her bed?"

"What? Maigrite Pickens, were you eavesdropping on my personal call?"

"Yes."

"Do you realize that's against the law?"

"Case you forgot, it's against the law to have personal calls here."

No longer feeling so chummy, Lou takes a step or two away. "I'm lactose intolerant."

"What were you doing in her bed?"

"Do you expect me to drive back to Brougham Gardens when I'm intolerant and no telling what might happen with my plumbing? I had to spend the night there."

"What's wrong with your husband's bed?"

"It's a twin. Not enough room. Don and I switched to Burma's bed last night. She used Don's."

"I see. So he's still living with that maid of his. In his own maid's house."

"For your information, Don does all the domestic engineering at Coffee Ridge. And furthermore, the only reason he's there is because I asked him to stay. To make sure *your* husband doesn't gain entrance to the premises."

"How thoughtful of you."

"Anything else you need to know?"

"Plenty else. But Lynda's buzzing me now."

As Maigrite limps into her boss's office, Lou's outrage seems to inundate every decent feeling left in her. But like a tuft of weeds, a certain hardy pity clings for dear life, a queer, useless, ragged love that survives the deluge.

Back at her desk, she sees that a fax has come through. An adminstrative secretary in the music department at St. Jude is asking for another set of evaluations from her former students. Lou sighs. It took her three days to unearth the first set in the attic at Brougham Gardens. Now they want another?

After a couple of sips of latte, though, Lou realizes this is a good sign. She's still in the running. She might yet find herself a respectable job.

CHAPTER TWENTY-ONE

Because the parish hall at Frederik Memorial is leaking—a yellow-pine limb crashed through the roof during the ice storm that paralyzed Tula Springs on Wednesday—the parish staff meeting is being held at Grady Morgen's. Lou, whose pen has run out of ink, can't help admiring her friend this evening. A twenty-year-old Chanel original gives Grady a severe elegance that makes Sting Courtney, the vivacious president of the Junior League, seem positively gaudy. As the butler glides into the room, Lou overhears Mary Ellen Shavers say something to Rowena Cobb about his sandals.

"Pipe down, Cobb," Grady says as Lou begins to read the minutes of the last meeting. Lou blushes for her friend's rudeness, but the provost herself seems unfazed. Lou speeds up as yawns blossom among the men. When it's over, she doesn't even note if the minutes are approved or not. She's lost in admiration. Never have the ceilings seemed so high, the ivy-leaf molding more splendid in its restraint. The lamps on the hunt table—she's never really noticed them before. They aren't things one could ever buy. You're either born with them or do without. Lou follows Sting Courtney's gaze as it wanders to the portrait of Judge Morgen's great-grandfather, painted by Joshua Reynolds's niece. Poor Sting—whenever Lou's been to her house for an Arts Council meeting, she's served shrimp fat as lobsters, fresh crab, baby asparagus, and, two or three times, caviar. She still hasn't worked up the nerve to imitate Grady's plain watercress sandwiches. With the crust left on.

When it's all over—a committee has been formed to look into a bazaar for the roof—Lou heads for the kitchen to retrieve the golf trophy she's sharing with Grady. Grady has had it an awfully long time, it seems.

"Dr. Jones," Rowena Cobb says as Lou totters in her cruel alligator heels atop a stool. She's reaching for the trophy, which is a hell of a way up on the shelves.

"Hey, Dr. Cobb."

"Good news. Crosby found a mortgage on the Web."

"You're kidding!" With the trophy jammed against her side, Lou is steadied by the provost's hand as she descends. "Oh, I know you're going to love it, Rowena. Brougham Gardens is really so convenient. Just look out the kitchen window and you can see what's playing, the feature times, everything. Then walk right over with your own popcorn. You'll save a fortune right there. And of course, the house itself, well, Don's really made it so original, the layout. You can pretend you're in SoHo."

"Crosby's not wild about the SoHo angle, that loft space. He's going to put in some walls downstairs. Make an actual dining room, living room, and close off the kitchen. Then he wants to tear out that sofa, all the built-in stuff you got there."

Lou blinks. "Yes, traditional rooms can be wonderful, too, in their own way. You can pretend you're in . . . New Canaan."

"What's that?"

"A suburb of— Oh, this? Just the trophy I won in that . . ."

"*We* won," Grady says as she breezes in with crystal stemware dangling from each hand.

"I meant *we*," Lou mutters lamely. Must Grady correct her in front of the woman who could hire her, Lou, at any moment? Especially after Rowena had just fired the head of the music department.

"Almost eight?" The provost frowns at her Rolex. "I told Crosby

I'd be home by seven. But Grady, you just tell me if there's anything I can do to help clean up even though poor Crosby must be
starving by now and . . ."

"These glasses." Grady sets the crystal in the sink and turns on
the tap. "Don't use too much hot water, either. I got to take a bath.
Lou, help me get rid of the watercress. Take some home with you."

"No, really, I couldn't . . ."

Grady herds Lou into the drawing room, where Bill is using a
broom to deal with crumbs on the threadbare carpet from Arbuth-
not Hall in Chipping Mare. The vacuum is too old and cumber-
some for most jobs. It takes more effort to put it together than to
actually vacuum.

"I heard, Lou."

"Fine. So shoot me."

"How much? What's the offer?"

Last week Lou had admitted to Grady what Rowena and
Crosby Cobb were willing to pay for the Brougham Gardens house.
It's too little, practically giving it away. But as Lou explained to
Grady more than once, she and Don simply can't afford to go on
dipping into their nest egg for the mortgage. No use throwing good
money after bad.

"You got Cobb up, Lou? Something in the ballpark of vague
sanity?"

"None of your business."

"And where do you and Don plan to move?"

"We'll find something, a nice, tidy little cottage. Really, Grady,
I'm so sick of Brougham. It's far too big. My heels actually echo
when I walk around in it. And we never use the pool. That potter
costs a fortune to pluck a few leaves out and— Stop, Grady. Please
don't." Grady goes on stuffing finger food into the trophy's cup.
"Don doesn't like watercress."

"Don't be silly, Lou. He'll like it. And you got to take some ostrich, too."

"What? The egg?"

"No, I made that skinflint husband of hers give me an actual
chick—hatched."

"Please don't tell me you've already butchered the poor thing. Oh, Grady . . ."

"Hardly. It's running around outside, having the time of its life. Cobb . . ." Grady nods toward the kitchen, where the water seems to be running full blast. "She brought ten pounds with her tonight. I wish she'd stop with the ostrich. Every time I turn around, she's pawning it off on me. Makes me ill, that meat."

Lou sighs. "Well, I suppose it'll be good for Don, his heart. Where is it? I want to get going. Got to get up at four-thirty tomorrow to do my bassoon column."

"Toolshed. Carla's out there now."

As Lou picks her way over live-oak roots breaching from the drenched loam, she begins to worry about the chick. Could be big as a turkey, and might pack a wallop with its beak. Hearing a rustling nearby, Lou clucks soothingly, hoping to assure it that a friend passes.

From the house, the toolshed looks far off. But she's upon it sooner than she expects. It's smaller than she remembers, when she and Grady used to play house here. Then it seemed a castle fit for Snow White. Now Lou can touch the cedar shingles on the steeply pitched roof. Burnished by time, they make the hut delightfully snug. Carla can work here, undisturbed. It's too hard to think in the main house, she's told Lou. Grady's always asking her where something is. Or the phone's ringing, or Bill's Mahler is blasting.

Lou raps with the brass knocker her father nailed into the oak. A dolphin from Bern.

"I'm really sorry to bother you," Lou says after the door opens with a somewhat fake-sounding creak. As if Peter Lorre lurked within.

Lou waits for a *good to see you, come on in, Louie.* But Carla goes right back to her laptop.

"Grady made me come out here to get some of that ostrich."

"The meeting over?" Carla says finally, leaning over toward the minirefrigerator. With a groan, she tugs, curses. The door finally opens.

Lou takes the lumps of bloody butcher paper from her. "This is so much."

"Go ahead. I can't eat it anyway."

As she works, Carla's long hair curtains the laptop's screen. The cot also serves as Carla's desk and chair. To get to the refrigerator and hand the ostrich to Lou, Carla didn't even have to unknot her lotus position. Everything she needs is right at hand. A saucepan steams on a hotplate in the recessed sill of the leaded window. Relishing the bouquet of jasmine tea, rain-soaked cedar, and something else—the bluets on the mantel?—Lou knows she should turn away. Leave the woman in peace.

"Watch out for Mrs. Tudie," Lou says, stepping over the granite threshold. "If she sees this place, she won't believe it's a toolshed. Just look at this fireplace, how all the stones fit without an ounce of mortar. And this marble sink in the bar—Carrara, Dad told me."

"Mm." Carla doesn't look up. Her fingers fly over the keyboard, efficient, relentless. Like Dame Myra Hess's tackling the *Hammerklavier* during the Blitz.

"She raised our taxes in Brougham Gardens, Mrs. Tudie did. Just last week she sent a notice about our toolshed. Simply outrageous, the final straw. Made us both decide, Don and me, that that was it—we've had it with that place. You know, Carla, you really ought to put some tools in here, a few shovels, a rake."

"Mm." Still not looking up, Carla gives her head an impatient shake, combs a free hand through the gray. The curtain parts. Lou can actually see the screen now.

"Women who sell out," the president of the Foreign Students Caucus averred on Friday to a packed house, "betray not only their own sex, but also every minority that struggles for its basic inalienable . . ."

Chilled by an almost sublime despair, Lou cannot read another word. With a stifled moan, she tosses the bloody package onto the cypress bar.

Still clutching her trophy, she totters off in her heels so precipitously that a trail of watercress is left beneath the ancient oaks. Headed for her car, Lou wonders about the slope, the way she seems to be going downhill. She's always thought Tula Springs was flat as a pancake. Yet she's going faster than she can manage really, close to foundering. Of course, this explains how Grady's house could seem one story in the front, and actually be three. The back of the house is on a slope. That's where all three stories are visible.

If so, where are they? Why doesn't she see the lights? Surely everyone couldn't have gone to bed by now. Bill's light would be on—the third floor. He's usually up till all hours, Grady says, blasting Mahler's Second, the *Resurrection*.

A hiss. Lou freezes. Could it be the chick, the baby ostrich? Too upset to cluck, she touches a rough trunk for reassurance, as if the oak could protect her. Another hiss.

"Numbskull," she mutters to herself. It's only the hiss of tires on the wet asphalt. There must be a street nearby, though she can't see anything yet. But if she's going toward the street, she's headed in the wrong direction. Yes, of course. She should be walking uphill toward the house. Not downhill.

"You really are a numbskull," Lou says aloud, giving herself courage. Walking in the wrong direction, toward the worst section of town, Hollywood, where they have those crack houses . . . "Moron."

"*Thanks.*"

Lou freezes, as if holding still will make her invisible.

"Here," Carla says, looming right in front of her. In her outstretched hands, the frozen ostrich. "Please. You'll be doing me a favor."

After a moment's hesitation, Lou takes the bloody paper. "I wasn't calling *you* a moron, by the way."

"I know."

The touch on Lou's forearm, light as a feather, is almost not there at all. Almost imagined. "Come back to the toolshed. Have some tea with me."

"I've got to get up at four-thirty tomorrow. My column. Tea will just . . ."

Lou yearns to go back there. It would be so easy to turn back. But she's afraid in that cozy hermitage, with the kerosene lamp flickering in the fireplace, she will be no match for Carla. Somehow the cook will persuade her that she is a Judas.

"What's with you, Lou?" Carla says when the lights of the house are visible. Mahler wafts through the grove of oaks.

"It hurts. It plain hurts. I'm not a sellout."

"Oh, Louise, stop with the martyr, will you?"

"We can't afford Brougham Gardens," Lou says, pausing by the garbage bins to catch her breath. "Don and I would go bankrupt if we didn't sell our house to the Cobbs."

"It's not about *you,* girl. That article is about Dr. Cobb. NOW is putting it on its Southeast Web site and . . ."

"Yes, and you'll be mentioning that house, I know. You're going to say I sold it to her so cheap because . . . Do you want to know the real reason? It's Mrs. Tudie and her pals on the zoning board. She's the one made the property almost worthless now with her movie palace and . . . Oh, never mind. You'll never see."

Lou tries to walk off. But the kitchen door has banged open. As Rowena Cobb heads down the outside stairs lugging a plastic garbage bag, Lou instinctively veers away from her. But not quickly enough.

"Lou?" Rowena calls out. "I thought you'd left."

"I have. But I had to get something first from . . ."

"Look, Louie," Carla says, ignoring the provost, who's stuffing the bag into a plastic garbage bin, "I really dig you. Despite all your politics, there's something I really like about you, see? I'm not going to hurt you."

"*Carla,*" Lou whispers, nodding toward Rowena, who's having trouble pushing all the garbage inside the bin.

"Come on back to the toolshed with me," Carla goes on, a shade louder. "I'll make you a hot toddy, help you sleep."

"Why isn't there a lid for this thing?" the provost says, turning from the bin. "Any decent housekeeper would have a lid."

In a few moments, Rowena Cobb is climbing the outside stairs to the kitchen door.

"Must you say things like that in front of her?" Lou demands, looking anxiously up at the kitchen window.

"Why are you so afraid, Lou? What can she do to you?"

As the contralto's *Röschen rot* pierces cleanly through the night, Lou clutches the trophy to her chest. "I want a decent job, Carla. Is that asking too much? I want some self-respect. I'm tired of . . ."

"Those con artists?"

"No, no, it's not them. That isn't my problem. They're good people, really. Look at all they've done for Grady. She's never looked better, so fit."

"But that Jesus business, Lou. It's really sick."

"That's not fair, Carla. Brother Moodie really believes. In his own way, he does. They've been good to me, too. All of them—except maybe for Maigrite."

"Who?"

"My supervisor. She's going through a rough time, Carla. Her husband just left her and she's anorexic, so I know she really doesn't mean to treat me so badly . . ."

"There you go again, Lou. First you say you hate your job and feel degraded and then you turn around and justify your own oppression. You make yourself a willing victim. That's what Alpha can't stand about you."

"But . . ." Lou feels a sudden wrench in her chest. The knot tightens. "That's so unfair. They're human beings, Carla. Maigrite, too. I can't help it if I really care for them. And after all I've done for Alpha, for her to say . . ."

"You've pitied Alpha. Just like that crazy woman, Mrs. Ompala. Well, girl, it's time to wake up and smell the coffee."

Lou's parked next to the provost's Mercedes SUV. Because of the gallery lights, it's not so dark here, easier to see Carla's face. The look is not quite as harsh as the words themselves. There's even a furtive tenderness at play in the eyes.

"*Me* wake up? All these years, Carla, I've tried so hard to get Alpha to be my friend. I've asked her time and again to have a cup of coffee with me. I've offered to pay for her education even though we don't have the money. If she just said one kind word to me, gave me a smile, a pat on the back, I could die happy."

"What's all that crap?" Carla's peering into the BMW, which Lou has just unlocked. Linens, books, a typewriter, olive oil, and CDs are strewn everywhere.

"I'm moving in with my husband," Lou says. "Going straight to Coffee Ridge tonight." Lou moves a can opener out of the way so she can sit down. "Why don't you look happy for me, Carla?"

"Do you really think it's such a good idea, Lou?"

"Living with my own husband?"

"I'm serious. I mean Burma's there, isn't she?"

"Oh, it's just temporary. Don and I are doing it as a favor for Alpha while she's away at the convention. We have to keep a sharp eye on Burma or she might wreck the house again. No nail sculptors, no superintendents. And you know we're paying Alpha, too. By the week. I wouldn't dream of it otherwise."

Lou hopes she sounds convincing. She really doesn't want to move back into Coffee Ridge. But since Don always comes up with one excuse or another why he can't move out, Lou has no choice. No husband of hers is going to share a house with a married woman on the cusp of divorce. Even if the married woman is extremely moral and over fifty. Appearances do matter, if not so much to Lou, to people Lou must deal with.

"I don't see why you and Don can't get a place of your own," Carla says.

"Well, of course we are. But Don hates to rush into things. He wants to scope things out first. So far all we've seen are huge spreads with five bedrooms or horrible plastic apartments. There's nothing in between."

"You'd think a small town like this . . . Oh, girl, just remembered. I've got to feed the chick. If he's not fed, he starts nipping at the dogs."

Before Lou can say good-bye, Carla has melted away into the grove. Looking out the rear window, Lou edges past the Mercedes. But then a sudden knock makes her slam on the brakes.

It's just Rowena, finally released from servitude in Grady's kitchen. She's rapping on the window.

"What's this?" the provost says after Lou powers the window down. She's pointing to the hood of the BMW. On it is the ostrich meat. Carla, who'd been leaning against the car as they talked, just left it there. Forgot to hand it back to Lou.

"Are you running off with Grady's ostrich?"

"No, I was just . . ."

"What's it doing here then?"

"I don't know."

"That cook was slipping it to you, wasn't she?"

"No, no. We were talking and she must have forgotten it or . . ."

"I'm going to tell Grady her cook tried to steal her good meat. The woman should be fired."

"Well, actually, Grady herself . . ."

No matter what she says, it sounds wrong to Lou, as if she's betraying someone. She really doesn't want to get Grady in hot water with Rowena. But at the same time . . .

"Grady absolutely adores it, Jones. Can't get enough. And people wonder why she's so thin, got such a great figure." As Rowena leans in closer, cicadas and Mahler blend with the purr of the idling engine. "So what's with you and that cook, Jones?"

"What? Me? I barely know her—really. I was just explaining that I can't eat ostrich."

"What's wrong with you?"

"Well, I mean—you know I'm Jewish and all."

"You're putting me on, Jones."

Rowena slaps her spiffy hairdo, a stylish pseudo-punk effect that Lou has tried to imitate, in vain. Hulga, her hairdresser, has a very limited repertoire. "I thought Grady told me your father was a priest or something. Had to flee from Germany because— Oh, you mean he was really Jewish, not . . . ?"

"He was a Catholic, Rowena. A seminarian."

"Then how can you be . . . I mean, your mother is a direct descendant of Jefferson Davis."

"On one side, yes."

"And on the other, that colonel."

"Right. So?"

"Old Blood and Guts Trott."

"Excuse me, but it was Trotsky, Colonel Trotsky."

"Oh come off it. Colonel Brent E. Trott—took a bullet for General Beauregard in Vicksburg—or was it Chattanooga? Anyway, he was about as Jewish as Beauregard himself. Owned a hundred slaves on his plantation—North Mississippi, right?"

"Who's been filling your head with all this nonsense? I never heard of anything more ridiculous."

"Grady said you could be elected president of the Daughters of the Confederacy just like that." The provost snaps her fingers. "I mean, if you ever joined . . . You haven't joined, have you? I really don't think as a serious candidate for a job at St. Jude you should . . ."

"Of course I haven't. I wouldn't dream of associating with anyone in that . . . Can't you tell when Grady's putting you on?"

"You mean she was making all that up? Shit, she got me again. I owe her one now, big time."

"Listen, Rowena, it's high time you learned to stand up to Grady. Don't let her get away with so much. Like the way she told you to be quiet tonight. It was really embarrassing."

"She was just playing with me, Jones. A little ribbing, that's all."

"Well, you shouldn't have done those dishes. Or taken out the garbage. I don't care how much Grady's given to those minority scholarships at St. Jude."

"Don't be silly. You take everything too seriously, Jones. And Lord knows Grady could use some help, what with that butler refusing to wash dishes and . . ." Holding up the bloody butcher paper, the provost makes a face. "Ugh. This meat's beginning to melt. Better get it back to Grady's fridge—pronto."

As Lou heads down the winding oystershell drive through the grove of oaks, she worries that she didn't make it clear enough that there was nothing going on between her and Carla. All that Jewish business got her offtrack. (The gall of Grady to make up stories about her, Lou, just to needle Rowena. And it's truly amazing how much a provost will tolerate from big-buck donors.) But to explicitly deny that she and Carla were having a fling, Lou would have sounded defensive, protesting too much. And besides, who could possibly think that someone as sleek and handsome as Carla Perlmutter would want to get mixed up with a dame like her, Lou? In fact, Lou feels a little flattered to be a suspect. Carla, after all, would be quite a catch for anyone so inclined.

CHAPTER TWENTY-TWO

"You fed a giraffe?"

"Look at this." Mrs. Van Buren holds up a lace panty that got slightly frayed coming out of the drawer. "Ruined. My mama might be able to fine-stitch this, though."

"What giraffe, Burma?"

Folding the panty carefully, Mrs. Van Buren says, "The one at the ostrich store. I wanted to buy Mama one of those music boxes they got there made out of ostrich. It's so hard to find anything for Mama's birthday. So I went clear out to that ranch and the lady who sold me the music box said I could carry the corn for the giraffe. That's what those things eat, corn."

"Don't yank, Burma. You'll ruin that one, too. Here." Lou gently removes another panty from the stuck drawer of the monstrous loblolly dresser.

"She's so beautiful, that lady," Mrs. Van Buren says after a vermeer-green panty is safely extricated from the drawer. "I don't think I ever seen someone so beautiful before."

Lou has been meaning to go visit Mrs. Ompala at Far Plains. But long ago when Rowena's husband gave a reception to welcome the giraffe's arrival on his ranch, Lou discovered she was allergic to Thomson's gazelles. Not just hives broke out during the reception, but she had terrible trouble breathing. Without the adrenaline shots in the emergency room, the doctor told her, she might have died.

"Were there any gazelles around?"

"Oh, yeah. I got to feed them some corn, too. And two emus . . . Oh, goody, Lou, you fished out my off-white. I thought it was lost."

Lou hands her the panty, which is carefully folded and stacked on top of the others. Thirty-nine down. Three to go.

"Alpha will be home on Sunday, you know." Mrs. Van Buren consults her watch, as if Sunday were only minutes away. "I don't see how you and Don are going to be moved out of here by then, Lou."

"Let's not concern ourselves with others' business, dear. Don is looking for a place this very minute."

"I'd say you could go live with my mama, only she's sort of particular about knowing people first, before they move in."

Lou takes a deep breath. "I hope Alpha's enjoying herself at the convention."

"It's a lot of hard work, she said. Hasn't been able to get herself much shut-eye. She's going to be plum tuckered out when she gets back and won't want a lot of noise, I reckon."

"Look, Burma, Don and I aren't the ones who make noise around here. If you don't mind my saying so, you seem awfully anxious to get rid of us. I hope this doesn't have anything to do with Mr. Pickens."

"Lou!" Mrs. Van Buren stomps a bare foot on the hooked rug. "I done told you I never let Mr. Pickens lay a finger on me. You've seen for yourself how I've thrown him out of this house three times already. Like when Dr. Jones brought him over for a drink so they could talk about y'all's toolshed. Try to get that tax changed."

"Yes, yes, I know . . . Don was totally out of line, and I let him know it, better believe. Well . . . Here's another. The last, I hope."

Mrs. Van Buren takes the final panty from Lou, who then tosses out the wire coat hanger they've been using to fish out the undergarments. The humidity has swollen up the dresser so bad that they can only open the drawer about a half inch or so. Even with Crisco.

"This dresser's been nothing but a headache from day one," Mrs. Van Buren declares. "Thank you very much, Mr. Pickens."

"Well, dear, you really shouldn't have accepted anything from a married man in the first place."

"I never accepted a blame thing from him. I just come home one day, and there it was, staring me right in the face."

Glancing anxiously out the bedroom window, Lou sees that the U-Haul has not backed over the Chinese cabbages that line the driveway. But it *is* headed straight for a push broom that lies, for no good reason, right smack in its path.

"Molly!" Lou shouts out the open window. "Be careful! My good broom!"

She can't bear to look. The snap nearly breaks her heart. "Don just bought it for me at the mall in Mississippi. For the anniversary of our first date."

"Don't worry, Lou. We got plenty of them at Freds."

"I don't think so. This was top of the line, Burma. The very latest engineering with a patented . . ."

"A broom's a broom."

"It *was* you, wasn't it? You're the one who left it smack in the middle of the drive this morning."

"Well, *excuse* me for trying to keep this place neat and tidy for Alpha."

"But the drive still isn't swept." Lou motions dramatically toward the window bedizened with Mrs. Van Buren's snap-on valance, whose ghastly florid loops can be changed with the seasons. "See?"

"Can I help it if the phone rings right when I start in on my sweeping? You want me not to talk to my own mama?"

"Your mama sounded an awful lot like Mr. Pickens this morning."

"You were easedropping, weren't you? Oh, I can't stand no more of this spying on me. I'm going to have me a conniption someday, I swear. "

Lou reaches for one of Don's handkerchiefs atop the loblolly dresser. It's been so hard having Mrs. Van Buren come into their bedroom every morning to fish out her panties with the coat hanger. Sometimes the woman plops down on the edge of the bed and chats with Don. Then she leaves her charm bracelets or Elizabeth Taylor on top of the dresser, forgetting that the bedroom is no longer her domain. Of course, this has put a strain on their relationship. But Lou believes that getting rid of the dresser will solve many problems. Mrs. Van Buren will no longer have any reason to come barging in, unannounced.

"Here, blow," Lou says, handing her the handkerchief.

Mrs. Van Buren wipes her eyes, then blows. "Thanks. I better let Grant and Molly in."

Lou sidesteps so Mrs. Van Buren can get past the double bed. "Now, Burma, let's make your friends feel welcome. A little sunshine." Lou demonstrates with a smile.

Molly, who repairs U-Hauls, and her partner, Grant, the librarian, have agreed to help transport the dresser back to Maigrite's. Such a time Lou had getting Don out of the house this morning. She simply can't afford any thoughtless words that might spark another incident like the fistfight. This was Lou's chance to smooth all that nonsense over, to show the girls that she and Don don't have an ounce of prejudice in them. Of course, it'll be easier to demonstrate this in Don's absence. Lou's sent him to look at a two-bedroom rental this side of Liberty.

"Whoa, this thing's a mothah," the librarian says after Lou compliments her, how comfortable her shoes look. "Don't think we're going to be able to get this mothah out the house."

"Now, Grant, honey," Lou says, "let's not be pessimistic. My husband has already been kind enough to remove the door. See?"

They all regard the empty space between the doorjambs. It's been this way since the dresser was moved in. Making love to Don on the Beautyrest has been a severe trial without a door. Especially with certain tenants wandering around with coat hangers.

"Molly, I declare that's the prettiest silk I've ever laid eyes on," Lou says after they've moved the dresser a few inches over the pine floor. And got a stray panty caught under it.

With a modest smile, Molly smooths a pleat. Not exactly the

most appropriate outfit for hauling furniture. But Molly has to pour at a Young Republicans tea this morning.

"I declare," the librarian echoes, in an exaggerated drawl.

Lou blushes. She never says, "I declare." What got into her? Oh, Lord, it's Maybelle. She's the one who always used to declare.

Grant puts her shoulder to the dresser, grunts. She, too, hasn't dressed very appropriately. Her vest has the most subtle weave, richly textured. How can a librarian afford something like that? Lou can't help wondering. And those shoes, they're exactly what Lou's been trying to find for herself. Only they never have her size.

Though Molly looks prim and proper, the girl knows her stuff. She positions everyone at just the right angle so that the impossible dresser slides past jutting corners. When Lou gets the strap of her overalls tangled in a bunch of carved loblolly grapes, Molly frees her with surprising ease. And when Lou's steel-toed Dickey boots are pinned by a sudden sag—"I can't hold on no more!" Mrs. Van Buren cried out—Molly comes to the rescue in a flash, somehow levering the weight off by herself. Lou is simply bursting with pride in the young woman.

"Where is Burma?" Lou says after the three of them have shoved, wedged, and tilted the monster all the way down the hall. "Where is that woman? Have we been doing this all by ourselves? Burma, Burma!"

Back in the bedroom, Lou finds Mrs. Van Buren perched on the window seat. Without the least bit of shame, Mrs. Van Buren gazes idly out at the street, just as if she were a great big pampered pussy, the darling of the household. "Burma, I think your friends might appreciate a little help. After all, this is not *our* dresser that's nearly killing us. You're the one who should be . . ."

"Shhhh."

"Are you shushing me? In my own house?"

"What's up?" Grant says as she and Molly two-step into the bedroom. Grant's got her arms around Molly's waist. They make a little circle of joy, pure joy, before Mrs. Van Buren says, "I think I saw him."

Entranced by the young women's delight, Lou forgets Mrs. Van Buren for a moment.

"Saw who?" Molly finally asks as their dance peters out.

"My husband."

"Burma, please don't start imagining things now," Lou says, striding over to the window. "You can at least wait until we get the dresser onto the truck."

"I'm not imagining. He went right by. I was slipping on some loafers so my toes won't get crushed by that blame thing, and I saw him. Plain as day."

Lou regards the tasseled Venetian loafers, Don's, that adorn the plump feet. Don got absolutely furious when Mrs. Van Buren forgot she had them on the other day and wore them to work. Lou hopes Mrs. Van Buren will forget again today and make them even wider, ruin them for good. Lou really can't stand them.

"You're telling me Mr. Van Buren just happened to stroll by?" Lou says.

"No. He was in his vehicle."

"His golf cart?"

"His Hummer."

"Well, lots of people could be driving around in a . . . What's a Hummer?"

"Believe me, Jones," Grant says, "you're not going to see that many canary-yellow Hummers in this burg."

"Lou. Please call me Lou. Well, Hummer or no Hummer, that dresser has got to be moved. Now come along, Burma. Look sharp."

Her eyes wide, lovelier than ever, Mrs. Van Buren has turned away from the window to gaze full blast at Lou. "Don't you understand? Mr. Van Buren hates me for moving out on him. He says he's going to kill me for ruining his life. Gun me down."

Pinning a cameo to her blouse, Molly says, "He better not try it while I'm around."

"Nonsense," Lou says. "I'm sure it's all talk. He's an elderly man, after all. In his eighties, right?"

"Eighty-one and a half," Mrs. Van Buren says.

Lou turns to Grant. "Is this on the level? You ever met him?"

Grant straightens the manager's name tag on Mrs. Van Buren's crisp outfit. "She does have a court order, Lou. I helped her get one. He's not supposed to come within ten feet of Burma."

"Ten?"

"We tried to get two hundred, but the judge was an ass. Said something about Van Buren's disability, how he has to use a golf cart to get around. Too proud for a wheelchair."

Lou turns back to the store manager. "Burma, did it ever occur to you that if you marry someone for money, then you might have to pay the piper?"

"Oh, Lou . . ." Mrs. Van Buren sags onto the window seat.

"Money?" Grant puts in. "The guy was just a catfish farmer about to declare bankruptcy when she married him, Jones."

"Yes, but . . ."

"The lottery came after."

"Still, for a young woman, a very attractive young woman, I might add . . ." Lou smiles in the direction of the window seat. "What business does she have marrying someone old enough to be her father?"

Her head between her hands, Mrs. Van Buren moans softly.

"Old Burm here"—Grant gives the name tag a pat—"she didn't realize he was twenty-six years older until it was too late. She'd already told him she was in love with him."

"I see," Lou says patiently. "That explains everything."

"They met in a chat room," Grant says. "He posted a picture that took twenty years off his waistline. By the time she saw how old he was in person, it didn't matter so much since she's not into looks."

"I'm not an ageist!" Mrs. Van Buren blurts from the window seat. She's peering out again. "People can't help it if they get old."

"She didn't know Mr. Van Buren was in a golf cart, either," Molly puts in. "He left that part out when they were in the chat room."

"Right," Grant goes on. "So when they meet, Van Buren says to Burma that most women are real prejudiced against folks that use golf carts. His own wife was before she passed on. She said the only reason he got himself one was because he was too lazy to pick his own nose. So Burma told him she didn't have anything against golf carts."

"I'm making Mr. Pickens put ramps in for him! All over town!"

"Burma, it's not necessary to shout, dear," Lou says.

"If marrying someone don't prove you aren't prejudiced," Mrs. Van Buren says more calmly, "I don't know what the heck does."

With a sigh, Lou picks a splinter of loblolly out of her hand. "And people wonder why I don't get a computer."

"Look, Jones, don't start dissing computers," Grant says. "How do you think I met Molly?"

"Well, I'm delighted everyone's been so perfectly matched," Lou says. "But this doesn't get the dresser into the truck. Now come along, girls."

"I'm not going out there," Mrs. Van Buren says after Grant and Molly have left the room. "You want me to get shot?"

"You ought to be ashamed of yourself, Burma. Talking that way about a poor, lonely old man."

"Poor! Who's the one bought himself a Tiger Woods with a built-in TV and bar—and cruise control? He's always watching *Wheel of Fortune* when he runs over my toes."

Lou settles down beside her. "You don't seem to get it, do you? That's just what marriage is about—having your toes run over time and time again. What you learn is how to keep out of the way, Burma. Sidestep. Or you buy yourself some good thick shoes. You don't go running around in bare feet."

"But I want him to have some feelings for me . . . Is that asking too much?"

"Dear heart, do you think a man that didn't have any feelings would want to gun you down? At *his* age, that's a lot of trouble to go through."

Mrs. Van Buren shrugs.

"Shouldn't that tell you something right there? I do declare, I think your husband really loves you. He can't stand being without you."

"But, Lou . . ."

"You're a Baptist, right? Remember how we were talking about the Old Testament the other night? When Carla came over for dinner? I was ranting on about how violent God seemed, how mad he would get at human beings. And what did Carla say?"

"Mr. Pickens and I quit believing in the Old Testament."

"Right. Just like the Nazis. They were the ones who wanted to throw out the Old Testament." Lou runs a finger through Mrs. Van Buren's silky blond highlights. "Burma, you know how good I think you are. You're one of those people who'll always do the right thing. Your moral compass won't let you . . ."

Mrs. Van Buren jerks her head away. "You're making me nervous, Lou. I don't like it when you start bringing up Nazis and morals."

"Just listen. Carla was saying all those stories in the Bible about God, how mad he got—well, it all goes back to one thing. He loves us so much. When you love someone so terribly, they can rip you apart when they . . . Oh, look. Can you believe?" Lou parts a fold in the velvet drapes for a better view. "The girls found that dolly. And look, Burma—they're trying to get the dresser up the ramp all by themselves. Oh, they shouldn't be doing that. We've got to go out there and help them. Come along now. Hurry."

CHAPTER TWENTY-THREE

As she clumps over to the ramp, Lou cries out, "Wait, girls! I'm here!"

With her shoulder to the dresser, she helps Molly shove while Grant, on the other side, tugs. In a few seconds, the dresser goes the final foot or two inside the truck.

"Girls, it's a miracle!" Panting hard, Lou gives them each a hug. "You've earned your crown in heaven this morning, I guarantee. Now all we have to do is haul this over to Mrs. Pickens's. You know where that is, Molly, don't you? Molly? Where are you going, child?"

"My coat. It's cold." The front door of the house opens, and Molly disappears inside. Mrs. Van Buren is still peering out the bow window, through the reflected nude limbs of a shivering crape myrtle.

"Give me a hand," Grant says. Lou takes an end of the quilted padding and helps drape it over the dresser's scrolls and carved grapes.

"You really are a wonderful friend to Burma, Grant. But I do wish you could talk some sense into her. Get her to see reason."

The librarian has settled onto the back of the van, her legs dangling over the edge. "Yeah, Jones, pretty awful, isn't it? Having a friend who refuses to be a gold digger. I've tried and tried to get that girl to see reason, to sell her soul to an abusive old crank who's half out of his gourd."

"Now, Grant, you know that's not what I mean."

"Well, then, just what *do* you mean?"

Lou wonders, would Mrs. Ompala answer such impertinence? Would anyone dare speak to Mrs. Ompala that way? No, because Mrs. Ompala wouldn't have got herself mixed up with a bunch of . . . Of people she doesn't know from Adam. Oh, why is Rowena Cobb taking so long to get her into St. Jude? Lou belongs there, with well-bred, educated colleagues who don't . . . *Why is that sweet gum wavering? Like a reflection of itself* . . .

"I mean," Lou goes on, as she steadies herself with the dresser, "I mean part of growing older, more mature, is to learn to honor certain commitments one's made. Now, I can see that a man like Mr. Van Buren may not be a barrel of laughs. But does that give Burma the right to ruin other people's lives? Maigrite's on the verge of a complete collapse, you know. I simply can't bear to see her suffer like this. Ever since Mr. Pickens left, Maigrite's been wasting away . . ." Lou glances at her Piaget. "As a matter of fact, I'm late. I should've been at the office long ago."

"If I were you, Jones, I'd keep out of this whole mess. Burma's always had a thing for Pickens. Yeah, the guy's a real herb as far as I can see. But Burma's able to see things in folks I wouldn't touch with a ten-foot pole. And it's all his fault, anyway. Burma never would've married the old buzzard if she hadn't been so hurt by Pickens. When Pickens got married to Maigrite, well, Burma just gave up, lost hope. She'd been thinking there was a chance Pickens and her might get hitched."

"Excuse me, Grant. We're talking about adultery here. Plain and simple. All these excuses we like to make for our friends don't . . . What's going on?"

The siren Lou's been trying to ignore has swollen to a triple forte. Wishing there were something to hold on to, she steps carefully down the ramp, which seems to waver worse than the sweet gum. Grant hops straight down.

"Good Lord," Lou says as Mr. Pickens emerges from his Miata. "What are you doing here?"

"Responding to a nine-one-one." He plucks a flashing light from the car's roof and stows it in the back.

"What? There's no emergency. Go away."

Pulling the belt of his London Fog a little tighter, Mr. Pickens consults his PalmMaster. "Call put in by a Mrs. Wentworth Adams III. Oh-nine-hundred hours this A.M., eighteen February."

"For heaven's sake," Lou says, vastly relieved. "You've got the wrong house. There's no Mrs. Wentworth Adams III here."

"Yeah, there is," Grant says. "Molly."

"What seems to be the trouble?" Mr. Pickens asks.

"Absolutely nothing is wrong," Lou says as quickly as possible. For Molly is emerging from the house in her red cashmere coat.

"Mr. Pickens?" Molly calls from the brick sidewalk with a near-sighted squint. "You know Burma doesn't allow you over here, Mr. Pickens. At least, not until you're divorced."

"Official business," Mr. Pickens says, flashing a badge pinned to the underside of his fur-lined coat. "AAA SecureCare. Mrs. Tudie dispatched me. Responding to a nine-one-one."

"Oh." Molly flattens the black-velvet collar of her coat. "Well, that's different. Burma's about to get shot, Mr. Pickens. You got to help her."

Mr. Pickens shakes his head sternly at Lou, who's opened his car door. She's gesturing toward the bucket seat with a pleasant smile.

"She's about to shoot herself?" he asks Molly.

"No, her husband."

"I see." With one hand he types on his PalmMaster. "Perpetrator is planning to shoot husband. Age?"

"Eighty-one," Molly says.

"No, ma'am. Perpetrator's age." Mr. Pickens arranges a gray lock over his bald pate. He coughs. "Age?"

"Hey," Grant says, yanking his sleeve. "Would you stop trying to find out how old Burma is? Besides, she's not the perpetrator. She's the victim." Grant snatches the PalmMaster and begins to type. "Mr. Elwood Van Buren planning to shoot Mrs."

"Give that back. I'm counting to three, Grant. One, two . . . Thank you. Now, Mr. Van Buren is in domicile with wife he's planning to . . ."

"He's not here," Lou says, wincing. A trilling in her temple threatens to erupt into a full-scale migraine. "Mr. Van Buren is not here, Pickens."

"How does he plan to shoot her then, Mrs. Adams?"

"A drive-by," Molly says.

Lou wonders what *Mrs.* Adams is supposed to mean. She hopes Molly is at least divorced. Or better yet, a widow. It'd be so much easier to accept Molly's help if her husband were dead. Oh, please be dead, Lou prays.

"Make of vehicle?" Mr. Pickens says.

"Hummer," Grant says. "Canary yellow. Burma said she saw it drive by just a few minutes ago."

"Is Mr. Adams . . . ?" Lou is asking at the same time. "Molly, is your husband . . ."

"Quiet, please," Mr. Pickens says. "One at a time. Now, Grant, what date would you put on it? A recent model?"

"Brand new. Every one of his nine cars is brand new."

"If I may talk now," Lou says, "I didn't see any Hummer drive by, Mr. Pickens. I think the whole thing is in Burma's head. She's just wishing he would drive by and take her back where she belongs."

"No Hummer? By the way, what's this?" He gives one of the U-Haul's tires a mild kick. "Who's moving?"

"No one," Molly says. "It's just that dresser Burma hates."

Mr. Pickens regards the quilted padding a moment. "And where is this being transported?"

"To your wife," Molly says. "I'm driving it over right now. You wait here, Mr. Pickens, and make sure Burma doesn't get shot."

"I beg your pardon," he says, starting up the ramp. "This happens to be my property. I paid three thousand dollars for this dresser."

Grant hoots. "You got to be kidding. This thing's not worth a plug nickel."

He's inside the truck now, inspecting under the padding. "Yes, this is mine all right. Y'all got to return this to its rightful origin in Burma's room."

"If you think for one minute, Mister, that I'm going to break my back lugging . . ." Lou swats her overalls. Her head feels as if it might explode. "This dresser is going the same place you're going, Pickens. Right back to *Mrs.* Pickens."

These turn out to be the last words Lou remembers saying— "*Mrs.* Pickens"—before that curious sting . . .

CHAPTER TWENTY-FOUR

Mrs. Melvin Tudie sticks the gladioli into a pitcher of ice water. Lou wonders if this is a good idea but doesn't say anything. The flowers themselves are a nice gesture. Mrs. Tudie didn't have to bring anything at all.

"How we doing?" Mrs. Tudie says yet again.

"We're doing fine. I'm not even sure why we're here. Seems like just a scratch."

"Observation, Lou. Can't be too careful with head wounds."

"But we weren't shot in the head." Twisting her arm back, Lou peers at the scar just above her elbow. After only two days, it's faded to a gentle rose.

"Yes, but Pickens reported that victim's head grazed ramp while fainting."

"The bump is gone, Mrs. Tudie."

"Dot. It's Dot. By the way, I tried to get you my room, Lou. I told the nurses you should only get the best."

"Your room?"

"Where I had my liposuction. And I've talked to my doctor. He said he could get at those thighs for you. Might as well, while you're at it."

Lou sighs as she motors her headrest up. Tri-Parish Pentecostal General was not her choice. She would have preferred the older, nondenominational hospital out on Martin Luther King Jr. Drive. But the ambulance was under a contractual obligation to take anyone it picked up to Pentecostal. And besides, Lou's health-care plan at WaistWatch doesn't allow a choice in the matter.

"Now, Lou, I do hope you've come to your senses," Mrs. Tudie says after offering her a Russell Stover chocolate, another gift from City Hall. Yes, Lou doesn't believe for one minute that Mrs. Tudie paid for the chocolate and flowers herself. "We *are* going to press charges against Mr. Van Buren, aren't we?"

"I've already told you, Dot. It was an accident. He thought I was Burma standing there with Mr. Pickens. The old man had no intention of harming me. He even sent me a get-well card." Lou reaches for it, lying atop *The Thin Red Line*. A tune erupts from it, *Happy Birthday*.

"Lou, Lou. We did bump our head pretty hard, didn't we?"

"If the pope, of all people, could forgive that Turkish man, then I think the least I can do as a . . ."

Mrs. Tudie puts a streamlined finger to her mouth. A nurse has come in to check the EKG monitor. After the nurse leaves, Mrs. Tudie says, "Not a good idea, mentioning the pope here. I wouldn't want your service compromised."

Lou smooths the coverlet atop her sheets. It has a strangely plastic feel, as if it came out of a mold rather than a loom. "In any case, Dot, you'll have to excuse me now. Thank you so much for the lovely flowers and that chocolate."

Mrs. Tudie doesn't seem to get the hint. Instead, she settles into the turquoise chair an inch from Lou's bed. "No hurry. Mr. Pickens is looking after AAA this afternoon."

"What about your taxes? Who's collecting them now? And who's superintending the streets and garbage? Honestly, Dot, I sometimes can't help wondering about City Hall."

"Don't worry that pretty little head."

"Well, I am expecting a phone call. Do you mind?"

Mrs. Tudie gestures toward the green phone. "Be my guest."

Handgun Control promised to call this afternoon. Lou wants

to be used for all she's worth. If only the woman would go, leave her in peace . . . But on second thought, it might be worthwhile for Mrs. Tudie to hear what she has to say. Why should Lou need any privacy for this?

"Hello, hello?" Lou says anxiously after Mrs. Tudie, who grabbed the phone first, hands it over to Lou and goes back to the *Marie Claire* that Mrs. Van Buren had left behind. "Ms. Plaice? Are you there?"

"Huh?"

"Oh, Grady. I was hoping it was Handgun Control. I'm giving an interview this afternoon. They're calling from Washington."

"What? Can't hear you, girl."

Braver now, Lou says boldly, in full voice, "Handgun Control."

The *Marie Claire* droops. But the perfectly made-up face, a little caked beneath the sagging, baleful eyes, is not aimed at Lou. It gravitates toward the TV, which cannot be turned off. Every room in the hospital gets free TV, twenty-four hours a day. "No good talking to *them,* Lou."

"I beg your pardon, Mrs. Tudie?"

"You were shot by a BB. Handgun Commies don't have any jurisdiction over toys."

"Toys? A rifle that could . . . Yes, Grady. Mrs. Tudie is here with me. I can't really talk now."

"Talk," Mrs. Tudie says with a blithe gesture. Her many charms tinkle.

"Lou, you there?"

"Yes, Grady. What is it now?"

"Carla wants to know if she can smuggle something in for you again."

"I've already eaten."

"It's a goulash we don't want."

"Gee thanks."

"Ostrich. Come on, Lou. She went to a lot of trouble."

"How am I supposed to hide ostrich goulash from the nurse? He's already fined me for eating that hummus Bill didn't bother to hide. And . . . Hold a sec. Yes, may I help you?"

An intern who came in to monitor the EKG is back again. A dour young woman, she wants to know why Lou thinks it's a good idea to put flowers in the ice-water pitcher. Lou doesn't answer at first, waiting for Mrs. Tudie to come clean. When the intern carries out the pitcher with the gladioli, Mrs. Tudie does get up, though, and follow her.

"Grady, listen—that reminds me. What's going on with you and Rowena Cobb? After the parish staff meeting the other day, she came out to the car and said the most idiotic thing. Really, Grady. You and she could benefit from some good counseling. I've never seen two women behave more weirdly."

"What the hell you talking about, Bear?"

"You know, the way you were teasing her about me. Saying I wasn't Jewish. It's not only disrespectful to Rowena—but to me. I really resent that."

"Bill, please turn down that Bruckner, will you? O.K., Lou, what? Resent what?"

"That ridiculous stuff you told her about Colonel Trotsky not being Jewish."

"Oh. So she blabbed. God, that woman. Can't keep a thing to herself. She swore up and down she'd never tell a soul."

"I don't get it, Grady. What's going on? Why do you confuse her like this?"

Silence.

"Grady?"

"The job. I went to see Rowena about the opening in the music department."

"For heaven's sake, I wish you wouldn't interfere. This is *my* business, not yours."

"Not just yours, Lou. Ever occur to you how it looks that the secretary of *my* parish staff works for WaistWatch? People talk. They say things about that place . . . They all wonder about you and Brother Moodie."

"They?"

"Sting Courtney and Mary Ellen Shavers and . . ."

Lou dabs at her eyes with a napkin plucked from the chicken-fried pork nuggets on her bed tray. "And? Go on, Grady. Don't stop there."

"By the way, have you heard the results of your MRI yet?"

"Don't try to change the subject. We've fooled each other long enough, Grady. Let's stop all this nonsense . . . It's you, you're the one who . . ."

"Don't, Lou. Don't go there."

"You're the one who's in love with Brother Moodie, Grady. And it's humiliating, right? Lord, the man wears white loafers and raps about Jesus. And won't give you the little affair that will tide you over until you find Mr. Right."

"Enough, Lou . . ."

"And you suspect that maybe *I'm* getting it from him. Can't stand that, can you, Grady?"

"That's a cheap, mean-spirited . . . After all I've tried to do for you, too." Grady's voice is choked, staccato. "All right, then. You want honesty? Rowena wasn't mixed up about you. I told her the truth, the God's honest truth. It's Trott—not Trotsky—just plain T-R-O-T-T."

Lou has to switch hands. The receiver is so thick, heavy as a dumbbell. "What?"

"He wasn't Jewish at all. Neither was your mother. She was a convert, Lou. That's why she worked for my father. Her family disowned her. She had to go to work when she was sixteen. Because she couldn't stand living with a bunch of stupid Baptist bigots who wouldn't even let her go to the funeral of her best friend. Because her friend, Anya Magda, was a Jew. And a rabbi was officiating. So your mother decided to teach her parents a lesson they'd never forget. She became a Jew herself."

The receiver sinks to the pillow. When Lou manages to lift it again, she says weakly, "Oh, God. Please, please don't tell me I'm really a . . ."

"Go ahead, say it, Lou. You're a Baptist. And your grandfather was a preacher, a goddam Southern Baptist preacher at a church that's still there. You can go see Ebenezer First Baptist in Burdin, Mississippi, anytime you damn please."

"Burdin? But . . . Grady, Grady?"

Nothing—only a dial tone now. Lou is trying to get an outside line—*busy, busy*—when the speckled gladioli return in a cut-glass vase. With Mrs. Tudie.

"Your pulse," Mrs. Tudie says, glancing at the monitor. "Lou, I'm getting a nurse."

"Don't. I'm fine. Leave me alone, please. I have to . . ."

"No, sir. Can't have this."

Before Lou can punch out Grady's number, Mrs. Tudie has returned to the room, an unfamiliar nurse in tow. Lou promises this nurse that she'll take the sedative later. A little later. But she is given no choice. Mrs. Tudie holds Lou's hand as the hypodermic stings the flesh just below the fading scar.

CHAPTER TWENTY-FIVE

The voices are saying how amazing it is, how fantastic. A miracle.

Lou opens her eyes. She wants to see this miracle. On the screen: 3 *Easy Payments (plus S&H)*. A bevy of young women in halter tops, every muscle in their abs defined, surrounds a gray-haired gentleman, so fit he almost seems computer-generated. The Ab-Wheel rolls, recoils. He stretches, he slims . . .

"Must you?" Lou says. Her mouth is dry, as if she's downed three or four Gibsons the night before. "So loud?"

Grady fiddles with the remote.

After gulping some water, Lou says, "Can't turn it off. Just mute. The little red button."

Grady finally manages this. She doesn't look well. A little haggard, as if she's been exercising too much without proper nutrition. Her face is drawn, ashen, like a biker's in a triathlon. Somewhat dazed, Lou reaches out to give her friend a reassuring pat. And squeals as a lurid tongue laps her hand.

"What in God's . . . Oh, Alice. It's you."

The mutt growls from beneath Grady's shawl.

"You can't bring dogs in here, Grady."

"She sorry, Horace." Grady nuzzles the shaggy face. "She no mean to scare you."

"If the nurse sees . . ."

"Relax. No one's going to see. And I wish you'd stop calling Horace a girl. It's going to give him a complex."

Lou regards her licked hand a moment, and then the Barbie doll, glistening with slobber, on her pillow. "Don't blame me, kid, if that beast has started playing with dolls."

"We're bad," Grady says, giving Horace a gentle spanking. "We steal Alice's Barbie."

Peering down at the mutt's wiry gray hair, rank enough to be smelled clear to the nurse's reception desk, Grady says, "I'm a bitch, Lou. A real bitch. I shouldn't hate you so much. So you've got everything I've always wanted . . ."

"Like this IV stuck up my arm? Or is it the botched MRI?" Water dribbles onto Lou's chin as she tries to sip at an awkward angle, so her hair doesn't touch the shiny doll. "Hold the hate, Grady. I don't have what you think. I really don't have him."

"But you just admitted on the phone . . ."

"Girl, I didn't admit a thing. I said it was stupid for you to *think* I was having an affair with Brother Moodie. I'm not."

Still contemplating the beloved Horace, Grady mutters, "Don't try to make me feel better. I can't stand that shit."

"Grady, look at me, I'm a wreck. I don't know what that nurse gave me, but I'm too stoned to lie."

"And you got that other hunk, too. Just adores you. Two, count 'em, two. And me? I'm so lonely I'm hoping to turn lesbian. But I can't even manage that. I'm just one big fat failure. A zero."

"Will you listen? It takes energy to lie—lots. I can't. Not now."

Grady sniffs, as if a suspicious odor lingers. "Yeah? How did you know, then? You must have had a good laugh, the two of you. When he told you how I asked for a ride home after class one morning, lured him inside. Tried to get him tipsy, actually snuck vodka into his grapefruit juice. Then spilled a bloody Mary on my dress, had to change . . . That must have given you two a big chuckle."

"Grady, honestly, Brother Moodie didn't say a word."

"Sure, Lou. Not a word." To the mutt: "She hear nothing, know nothing."

"I was just guessing."

"Some guess. Tell me this, Lou—did you know that night? Did you know he'd been over that very morning, before Mrs. Ompala came to dinner?"

"You mean the night of the recital, Cheryl Ames's recital?"

"I couldn't believe what an ass I made out of myself. With him. In my bathrobe, parading around in front of him, then . . . Then . . ."

"He hugged you? Period?"

The bitterness on Grady's face seems oddly familiar. "So he did tell you, Lou. Well, hope you're satisfied, friend. Must have given you a big charge."

"No, Grady. I . . ."

"And you've known all along what a fool I am. Even that night with Mrs. Ompala when I was trying so hard to forget . . ."

"No, Grady, I never knew a thing. Honest." Lou wishes she could stop here and still be plausible. Why must she go on? Why can't Grady just take it on faith that she's too exhausted to lie? But there seems to be no other way out. She must go on. "Brother Moodie hugged me, too. And that was it. Just a hug. He never mentioned a word about you. I was only putting two and two together."

"You mean you never knew he came over before Mrs. Ompala?"

"No, I swear I . . ."

The nurse pokes his head into the room. "How we doing?"

Lou tries to say something, to explain that she really has nothing to do with the dog on that woman's lap, but the nurse is gone before anything comes out.

"Maybe he thought Horace was a muff," Lou speculates before they return to Brother Moodie. As fierce as her pride, Grady's skepticism makes her probe relentlessly. Lou is forced to give details of her own encounter with Brother Moodie after Grady swears not a word of this will get back to Don. It feels wrong, somehow, having to admit how awful she felt during the bunion lawsuit. She was so depressed that she hoped only to curl up and die one day, without any more of the constant, drumming anxiety, the panic attacks. And then, he held her. He reached out and took her in his arms. She could lean against him. Entirely.

"Oh, Lou, I had no idea how bad that bunion business was. You never said anything to me about . . ."

"It wasn't just that. The depression was worse, really. Much worse. There wasn't any meaning in my life. None. Everything seemed turned upside down. I couldn't trust anyone, anything. Not even myself. I had so many crazy thoughts. God seemed so cruel, so unjust and . . ."

"I know, girl. I know all about it. Get that way myself."

Lou is reassured. Grady really does seem to believe that she, Lou, hasn't been unfaithful to Don. But there's still a queasy sense that something is wrong, terribly wrong. Then, as Grady begins to go on about a session Horace just had with a behavioral therapist, Lou remembers. She has lost something terribly important, the very core of who she is.

"But, Lou, you *are* Jewish," Grady tries to reassure her. "Just because there's no blood connection. It's all about faith, isn't it? Your mother made that leap of faith."

"*She* did, yes. I didn't."

"But it counts for you, too." Grady has set Horace down and perches on the edge of the hospital bed, holding Lou's hand. "And besides, you made your own leap when you got baptized."

"I don't know, Grady. Somehow it just doesn't feel right to me now, being Christian without . . ." She feels herself sinking under some irresistible, wonderful weight. "Without first being a . . ."

"Don't try to talk now, Lou. Take it easy."

"I mean, unless you know what it feels like . . ." Her eyes try to remain open. But the lids are so heavy. They just want rest, blessed rest. "To the core of your bones, what it feels like, then I don't think you can ever really know what . . ."

"Sleep, Bear. Sleep."

"I thought I knew, Grady."

"Stop with the worry, Bear. Sleep."

"I really thought I knew . . ."

Lynda sways with the palms, erect, but leaning slightly forward, beckoning the sea. The color needs adjusting. The fronds have a bluish tinge, and Lynda seems somewhat leached, like driftwood, paler . . . Her island seems less beautiful. Grady should do something with the remote. Do something . . .

"What?"

Lou, fully awake now, hopes she didn't say anything embarrassing. "Still here?"

"Got in a little workout." Grady stops stretching with the exercise video, which plays at least three times a week on the parish cable station. This had been Lou's idea. When she helped with the Christmas-parade broadcast, Lou had found out that the station was running out of product to air. So she volunteered Lynda's video. And they were glad to have it, even though at the end of every half-hour segment there was an ad for WaistWatch. Free advertising. Brother Moodie, of course, was delighted by Lou's enterprise.

"You don't look so good, Lou. Are you sure that bullet . . ."

"My head. That's what they're worried about. I hit my head on the ramp of the U-Haul." With a groan, Lou tries to sit up. "Any word yet? The MRI?"

"No one's been in. Want me to go check?" Grady powers the bed so Lou is more upright. "Better?"

Lou nods. "But don't check. I don't really want to know anything more. Not now. I've had enough for one day."

"Is it really so awful finding out you're not Jewish?" Grady says, mopping Lou's damp brow with a napkin. "I didn't mean to hurt you, girl."

"All this time you've known. And you never told me."

Grady retreats to the turquoise chair under which Horace

naps. "The judge made me swear, Lou. My dad made me swear I'd never tell you. That's what your mother wanted."

"Then why the hell did he tell you?"

"Lou, calm down. Your pulse is really not good. The nurse told me you've got to take it easy."

"Why? Why couldn't your father just keep it to himself?"

"He tried. But I overheard something one day. And he had to explain to me afterward. See, my mother was giving him hell one day, right after the funeral, your mother's. She discovered the bill from the funeral parlor. He had paid for everything—and Mother was livid. She was saying how she wouldn't be footing the bills for every little Baptist floozie he drags in her house."

"He paid?"

"Yes. My dad did love your mother. He respected her so much. Mother was screaming so loud at him, I couldn't help hearing. She accused him of sleeping with your mother. God, was she jealous. She called your mother a dirty, gold-digging trailer-trash Baptist. He had to explain to me then—I mean, since I always thought she was Jewish. I couldn't understand why my mother called her a Baptist. Dad couldn't bear to have his secretary's name dishonored. There was never any funny stuff between them, Lou. He wouldn't have dared. She was the most courageous woman he'd ever known, he would tell me. Really noble. And I believe him, Lou. There's no doubt in my mind. Because there were others, floozies, like I said. And as you know, your mother never got a cent from my father besides her salary. She wouldn't even let him pay more than the going rate for clerical help. She demanded only what was fair."

Lou's head sways wearily against something dank. She tosses Grady the Barbie on her pillow.

"Oh, Lord," Lou says, her eyes drifting back to Lynda on the pink sands. "What will Don say? All these years he's loved me because he thinks I'm . . ."

"Hey, he loves you for being you. Period. And besides, who says Don's got to know?"

"It'll get out. Rowena . . ."

"Don't worry about her. I already called her up before I came over this afternoon. Read her the riot act."

Lou, still groggy, motors the bed higher. "I still don't understand why you were talking about me to her anyway. It's none of Rowena's business."

"Here, baby! Yes, here! Look what Mommy has for you!" Grady dangles a pork nugget over the edge of the turquoise chair. Horace looks up with dim, world-weary eyes, sniffs, and goes back to sleep. "Didn't I say about that job, that theory position at St. Jude?"

"That doesn't explain why you had to go into my background like that."

"If you knew about Rowena, you'd understand. In the Sixties she was on a bus with civil rights workers from Maine, came all the way down here to help with voter registration. Went through hell, poor girl. A clerk of court spat in her face, then she was thrown in jail."

"The clerk?"

"No, Rowena—for delivering a left hook upside the clerk's beehive. Served three months for assault and battery. Rowena was so glad to get out of Eutaw alive. This was right after those murders in Philadelphia . . ."

"It was Eutaw?"

"Yes, our dear mall. Actually, before the mall. Anyway, I drove down to St. Jude to ask Rowena what she could do. If she could help swing things your way for that job."

"Girl, you must stop sticking your nose into my business," Lou says after a weak groan. There's a straw in the glass now, so it's easier to sip the water. "What did you do, offer her another one-point-three million if she hired me?"

Grady stops stretching her legs with Lynda and looks around. "You're not supposed to know about that, Lou. Who told you?"

"Who do you think?"

As one of her first projects at St. Jude, Rowena had started a minority scholarship program. When she had come to Lou for a contribution several years ago, she mentioned that Grady had contributed a mite or two. One-point-three million, to be exact. It shamed Lou and Don into making a much larger contribution than they could afford.

"Did you offer her a bribe, Grady?"

"Not a cent, I swear."

"Well, that's a relief. But then you go on and tell Rowena I'm not really Jewish? How does that help? Wasn't her uncle or cousin or something a rabbi?"

"I know, I know. I just wanted Rowena to find out how brave your mother was. That there were Southerners who weren't like those cretins in Eutaw. I was telling her how Baptist your mother was to show that someone with a lineage like that, you know with all those Confederate colonels in the family . . . Well, I was going to tell her how your mother turned her back on all that. She was so disgusted with the way her father and mother treated this friend of hers that . . ."

"What friend? And what do you mean, you were *going* to tell Rowena."

"Rowena's a very busy woman, Lou. I really couldn't get the whole story across. She was always being interrupted by calls in her office, assistants walking in and out. I'm not sure she was even listening to everything I did get to say. And then, after she broke me off in the middle of the story, she was in China teaching advanced PowerPoint. I didn't see her for months afterward."

"Many thanks. So she hears the part about my mother's parents, the horrible Baptist preacher and his wife."

"Oh, Lou, your mother's story wouldn't make any sense unless I set it up first, described what she came from."

"Promise me, Grady. No more favors. Let me get my own jobs."

"Well, I didn't believe you were so innocent, Lou. I wanted you out of WaistWatch. You can't blame me for that."

"Why can't I? I told you I wasn't having an affair. Remember when you were helping me paint the handicapped space? I said it plain as day."

"What are you supposed to say? Of course you have to deny it. That only confirmed everything I suspected."

Once again, Lou is forced to go over the same territory to prove her innocence. It's amazing how stubborn Grady can be, how she can doubt a friend who has bared her very soul.

After Grady's faith is restored—somewhat—Lou can get back to her real question. What friend?

"Anya Magda," Grady says. "She could barely speak English. Your mother took her under her wing, tried to help her with her homework. Anya Magda suffered terribly in high school there, in Mississippi. She was Jewish, the only one in school. She was living with her grandparents in Burdin. Her parents had died, both of them, in Budapest, and Anya Magda had emigrated, alone."

Some knot in Lou's breast relaxes. For the first time, in so many years, it seems, she can breathe properly. "Anya Magda. My namesake. Mother named me after . . ."

"She was never well, Lou. Anya Magda had rheumatic fever. When she was sixteen, she died. It was a terrible blow to your mother. But what made it worse, her parents wouldn't allow her to go to the funeral. They had always given Louise grief about her friendship with Anya Magda, wouldn't allow the girl in the parsonage. And when they heard a rabbi from Memphis would be officiating at the funeral, well, your mother was locked in her room.

"It was then, during the funeral, alone in her room, that your mother decided to convert and tacked a 'sky' on her name. When she told her parents, they kept her locked up, no school, no visitors. But she managed to escape. Your mother stole twenty-six dollars from the collection, what was going to buy a Confederate flag for her father's church. And she got on the Greyhound, left Burdin. Tried to get south to New Orleans, where she knew there would be some Jews. But she didn't have enough money to make it all the way. She ran out in Tula Springs. That was where she got off. Had to get a job at a store, the bargain store."

"Not Sonny Boy? My own mother? There?"

Grady nods. "Dad came in one morning looking for a drain guard for his sink. And he knew right away, talking to her, that this young woman was far too bright to be wasting her time there. He hired her on the spot, Miss Trotsky, as his secretary."

"Sonny Boy?" Lou says, still dazed by an exquisite pain, so poignant it almost seems beautiful. "She worked in Sonny Boy?"

"For a while, yes." Grady sighs. "Oh, Horry, Horry, what has you done, silly baby?"

Lost in wonder, Lou doesn't hear the fuss Grady is making now about Horace, who has swallowed something white on the floor. While Grady tries to make the mutt cough it up, Lou marvels how all these years she has carried this name, Anya Magda, a whole history, without feeling the slightest burden.

CHAPTER TWENTY-SIX

"Go home."

"Quiet."

"Please, go home, Don. Get yourself a decent night's sleep."

But he doesn't put down the turquoise chair. After wheeling the IV stand aside, he wedges the chair by the radiator. The cot can now be fully opened. Somewhat mesmerized, Lou watches as he squares the corners of the sheets. They do indeed look as if you could bounce a nickel off them. It could have passed inspection at The Citadel, if the academy allowed black satin sheets.

The first night he stayed over was touching. But it was so hard for Lou to sleep. It wasn't so much his snoring, but his anxiety. She could tell this ordeal was worse for him than for her. Although she really could forgive Mr. Van Buren, Don was still filled with vengeance. He was worried, too, that Mr. Van Buren was unbalanced enough to plan another attack on Lou.

"But I'm not his wife," Lou had tried to reason the day before. "You should be at home protecting Burma."

"Burma doesn't need any protecting. Not with that mother of hers around."

Burma's mother has bivouacked at Coffee Ridge to keep her daughter safe after the drive-by shooting. And apparently, Don and the mother don't get along too well. They've already had words. Mrs. LaSteele, the mother, had bought a lamp at Wal-Mart for her bed table. When she complained that the lightbulb was too dim, Don screwed in a new one, and the lamp went on the fritz. It was only made to accommodate Chinese lightbulbs, Mrs. LaSteele informed him. Don had screwed in a U.S. bulb and of course should reimburse her for the ruined lamp.

"How long does she plan to stay?" Lou asks mildly from the raised hospital bed. "Don?"

He's sitting on the edge of the cot, removing his patterned socks. "The old bat? Until he gets out of the hospital."

"What? Who's in the hospital?"

He blows on the socks before folding them neatly together. "Look, Lou, I didn't want to alarm you. But there's a real reason for me to be here with you. That nut case is here, in this very hospital."

"Pickens?"

"Van Buren. He's having a quadruple bypass. Apparently, all the excitement was too much for him."

Lou ponders this a moment. "I'm so sorry. Really sorry."

"There you go again."

"What? Can't I feel sorry for a disabled eighty-one-year-old having a bypass? Now, Donald, I do hope this will put an end to all this nonsense about pressing charges against him."

"You kidding? If you don't, better believe I will."

This was, at least, an improvement. Before Mr. Van Buren's admittance to the hospital, Don was threatening to blast out all the windows in Van Buren's Graceland II with his shotgun. Pressing charges was one small step in the general direction of adulthood.

"Dear, if Mr. Van Buren is safely in the hospital, why is Burma's mother still in the house? And please don't call anyone's mother an old bat."

"Because she doesn't trust me to keep Pickens away. Burma's mother is worried to death about her daughter's reputation. She's determined to get Burma back with Van Buren."

"What? Is she crazy?"

Don slips a gray satin pillowcase over the foam rubber. "Mrs. LaSteele doesn't believe in divorce. She's a very strict Baptist who's tooling around now in a freshly minted Cadillac, top of the line, with a built-in cell phone and minibar."

"What?"

"A gift from her poor, sickly son-in-law, who was aiming at Mr. Pickens, not Burma—or you. Poor Mr. Van Buren saw the U-Haul parked out front and thought Pickens was moving in with his wife. The old man had no intention of plugging Burma, wouldn't ever have dreamed of it. He was after the home wrecker. But his eyesight's not the best these days."

"I see."

As her husband slips off his trousers, Lou relishes the lavish floral arrangement from WaistWatch. Amaryllis and lilies predominate, but there are more modest flowers she can't identify. The delicate whorls, the way the petals seem fraught with the bluish grays of a late winter sky . . .

"It's odd, Don. No one from work has come by. I was sure Maigrite, at least . . ."

"Where's my slippers? Did that nurse take my slippers again?"

Regarding him as he too studiously peers under the turquoise chair, Lou says, "They did come, didn't they? Look at me, Don."

"All right. So they tried to barge in. You were sleeping. I told them you needed your rest. Can't have too much excitement."

"I wish you wouldn't play watchdog like that."

"I let Mrs. Tudie in."

"Gee, thanks."

The slippers are right by the cot. He doesn't put them on. "And Grady."

"Who came, Don? You said they."

"Mrs. Pickens. And Brother Moodie's little harem."

"What about him? Did he . . ."

Don shrugs. "Elmer Gantry was here. Amazing how his girl-friends can't do anything about his wardrobe. They fix up everyone else in town. Him, he looks like trailer trash."

"Don!"

"Don't 'Don' me. I let him know what's what. Said you wouldn't be requiring his services any longer."

Lou motors even farther upright. "Dear heart, what sort of crazy talk is that?"

"You quit. I let him know you were sick and tired of working for his loony Jesus freaks."

"But . . ."

"Look where it's landed you, Lou. In a hospital that can't even do a decent MRI. You have to take it over again, you know."

"Yes, yes, I know. But that isn't Brother Moodie's fault."

"If you hadn't been at WaistWatch, you'd never end up being shot, Lou."

"By a BB, a toy."

"Baloney. You realize how easy you could've had your eye put out? I tell you, I've humored you as long as I can. Enough's enough."

Lou tries to speak. But her throat is too tight. Almost panicky.

"Here you are with a Ph.D. playing maid for a bunch of Baptist sexpots . . ."

"Maid?" Lou manages to croak out. "Who said . . ."

"Grady told me you clean their toilets. She's seen you."

"I never . . ." Lou sips through the straw. "Once I unclogged a toilet. Once. Maybe twice."

"And painting their parking lot. That bum made you paint in all the handicapped spaces, didn't he?"

Lou sets down the plastic cup of water. "Is that all, Don? Is that all she told you?"

"That's enough for me, babe. More than enough."

The Pentecostal mattress crackles as he settles in beside her. When she tries to shift away, he pulls her to him. Firmly, yet gently. The intravenous drip—*Why is it there? What is it for? Don't ask, don't tell*—is not disturbed.

"You know how much I love you? Look at me, Lou. You know I'd do anything for you."

"Let me rest. I'm so tired."

"If I had stayed home, if I hadn't gone out to look for a house— oh, babe, I could've taken that bullet for you."

As he strokes her matted hair, Lou tries to work up some righteous anger. He can't quit for her. That isn't right. But she's too weary now. She makes a mental note to be angry later, when she has her strength back. For the time being: "That BB was good for me, Don. Finally got me to a doctor, didn't it?"

"You've been a very bad girl."

Yesterday, Lou had admitted to Don that for the past year or so—maybe two, three—she'd had scheduling conflicts with her doctors. Several appointments were postponed because she was so busy. Or had forgotten. You'd think the nurses might have called to remind her, though. Why should she have to think of everything?

"I would've had the stroke anyway, Don. My blood pressure was so high. My cholesterol . . ."

He squeezes her hand hard. "Don't say that, Lou. No one knows for sure you had a stroke. Not yet. You're going to come out of this with flying colors, I guarantee."

"Sure, honey."

It's too awkward for them to look directly at each other. Side by side they lie, talking to the ceiling. In her peripheral vision, he is flattened, somewhat more russet, like an apple by Cézanne.

"You will. You're a survivor. Think of all your people have gone through. This is nothing. You'll pull through."

"My people?"

"Why do you think I fell for you? You were so different, Lou, such a breath of fresh air. I mean, how many cheerleaders could whip out a bassoon and play Hindemith—from memory? God, it pisses me off when I hear some dumb redneck let loose with a . . . You realize how many noses got bloodied? Beat the crap out of Cutrer once."

"Rodney? Most Handsome?"

"The little coonass made a crack about Goldwater, called him a kike. If Coach Fox hadn't come out of the dugout and broken us up . . ."

"Goldwater wanted to use nuclear bombs on Vietnam. Couldn't you have found someone more . . . ?"

"I don't care if he was planning to nuke Vegas. No one's going to use that word around me."

Lou adjusts the IV line running into her arm. "So that's all Grady told you? Toilets, the parking lot? Nothing else?"

"Why do you keep on bringing her up? She just told me I did the right thing, that's all. Getting you to quit."

"Don, why don't you go over there and sit down, hon. There's something I want to tell you."

"Tell me here."

"No. I need some space. Give me some space for this."

CHAPTER TWENTY-SEVEN

He's snoring on the cot, a satin sheet drooping to the linoleum.

She has told him. All. Everything she knows. But this everything—what was passed on from Grady, who was retelling what her father had told her, and his tale but a version of what he had heard from Lou's own mother—is, in the end, so little. How much did her mother leave out when she told Judge Morgen? And how much did Judge Morgen forget when he told his daughter? Or slant in a certain way?

Light filters through the satin pillowcase Don taped to the television screen. He had tried in vain to turn off Lynda, who slims to Caucasian rap among the listing palms.

Colors bleed through the satin. Shapes flicker upon a wall until it seems to Lou, tranquilized upon the bed, somewhat believable that every solid, as Don once tried to instruct her, is mostly space, the enormous space between nucleus and orbiting electrons. Other rooms open up from this, where she has been confined so long. At the end of a long hall, an archway. And beyond this, a courtyard. In her mother's home, Burdin. That raw north Mississippi town Lou visited once. She never really knew why she was invited there to speak to the children. About music, the family of wind instruments. Who remembered her? Who was asking her back? She was almost a native—and didn't even know it. She didn't know the alien ground she walked upon was actually her own soil. She couldn't see how lovely Burdin was . . . Until now. Peaches hang ripe, luscious, dusky in that courtyard. Beyond are crenelations, towers, ramparts.

Lou must suppress an urge to wake Don. To show him those peaches. Anya Magda, her namesake, is feeding one to a goat. No, not just a goat. The noble head turns and she sees the slant golden eyes of the East. The horn a cornucopia. It is a ram's horn.

She offers one to Lou's mother. Louise takes the dark peach. Anya Magda and Louise are both sophomores. They share a world that is more beautiful than anything Lou could ever imagine. Because it is energy. Which is delight. In the distance, the naive distance before the laws of perspective, is the castle. Lady Fitzhoward awaits. She will dance beneath the yew. The ram and the ewe will lie down together.

When Lou is nudged awake, she doesn't remember at first. All she feels is a joy that aches so badly, she must hug him. "Oh, Don, Don . . ."

"Uh, actually, it's like me."

With some effort, Lou manages to pry her heavy lids open. "Bill? What are you doing here, honey?"

"Wanted to say good-bye. I'm off to L.A."

"What time is it?"

As he lifts his thin wrist, the chromium watch made in the German Republic slides down his arm.

"Seven something. Don's got the feedbag on downstairs in the cafeteria, his oats. I'd rather not run into him. That's why I woke you. Hope you don't mind, Miss L."

"Miss L. doesn't mind."

He stands there uncertainly, first on one foot, then the other.

His shirt balloons around his waist. But it is pressed. And smells fresh, so fresh, even from the bed. "I sold a script finally. Going out for a story conference."

"Good, darling. Your father must be proud."

"Well, he's not really into *Fear Factor*."

"What's that? I thought you were doing something about the news."

He lifts his shades and peers at the amaryllis. "Someone from *Inside Edition* got hired away by *Fear Factor*, and like you know . . . By the way, congratulations."

"What? For getting shot?"

"The job. You got the job."

"St. Jude? Oh, no, Bill, you must be mistaken. I haven't heard anything yet."

"You will. Alpha told me it's in the bag. You're in."

Lou dabs at her eyes, still encrusted. A reaction to the sedative. Every morning it's so hard to clear her eyes. "Alpha? How in the world would she know?"

"I'm not supposed to tell." He twists a gelled cowlick. "I promised Alpha I wouldn't."

"Look, kid, I'm on my last legs. Your secret is safe with me."

"Come on, Lou. It was just a BB."

"Tell me. Please. I must know."

"You know that convention Alpha went to in Shreveport? Well, they passed a resolution. By a vote of 189 to 188, Rowena Cobb was given the official support of the Western Chapter of the AARP Student Caucus. It's the umbrella group for Alpha's own caucus. So Dr. Cobb told Alpha that because of this show of confidence she's going to give you a clean bill of health. All along, the music department's wanted to hire you, but Dr. Cobb was afraid of another outburst on campus. She's a little gun-shy after all that uproar about Dean Whitney. So you see, Alpha's actually with you now."

"But the other candidate, is he . . . ?"

A candy striper wheels in a tray of books and magazines. Lou selects a biography of Jimmy Swaggart. On his way out, the candy striper says he's gonna have to tell on that man there. These aren't visiting hours yet.

Craning his neck for a last look at the candy striper, Bill says, "He's from England. He's having all sorts of difficulties getting a green card for the job."

Lou motors the bed a few degrees forward. She's been looking at Bill from an odd angle, a certain foreshortening that makes his chin too large. It helps restore a sense of normality, this new position. "But Bill, what if he's African-American? I'm not sure I'd want this job. Imagine what a fuss there'll be. I can't stand any fuss now."

"Relax, Miss L. He's English—period. That's all you need to know."

Lou ponders this a moment while he fiddles beneath his shirt. "Before you go, Bill, would you do me a favor? Would you please find out how Maigrite is doing? I've been so worried about her. Don won't let her come see me and . . ."

From beneath his shirt, Bill brings out a plastic container. He puts it on her bed tray, beside an uneaten supper.

"Goulash, Bill?"

"Carla made me. She's determined to get rid of that ostrich."

"It's frozen."

"There's a microwave right down the hall. Just pop it in."

Lou holds up her IV'd arm. "Do I look like I can pop anything in? Oh, well. Don can eat it."

"Why aren't you eating, Miss L.?"

She pinches the sagging flesh beneath the BB scar. "I'm finally losing weight, Bill. Don't knock it. I'm getting back to my old self again."

"Grady's worried. So's Carla. You got to eat."

Lou takes a sip of water. Her mouth is so dry all the time. She can never get enough water, it seems. "What about Maigrite, Bill? Will you go see about her?"

"Don't have time. My plane leaves in a couple of hours. Anyway, she's fine. Pickens has moved back in with her."

"Oh, how wonderful."

"Yeah, wonderful. Grady told me that his half brother kicked him out. Couldn't stand having Pickens around the house all the time."

"Well, the important thing is that he's back with her."

"He had nowhere else to go, Lou."

"Yes—what better reason could there be?" A weight seems lifted. Lou breathes more easily. "Well, if you're in such a rush . . . Or are you waiting for that candy striper to evict you, Bill?"

"Ha. Very funny."

"Dear child . . ."

"Huh?"

I'll miss you, she tries to say as he shoulders his knapsack. But her mouth is too dry, and he leaves.

CHAPTER TWENTY-EIGHT

The new charcoal pantsuit she bought at Lane Bryant next to the Bulgar Service Number One is in the backseat. Lou is still worried about her stomach. She doesn't want to get on a stretch of highway where there is no possibility of a restroom. It's somewhat daunting how much space there is between towns in Mississippi. You can drive for miles and miles before hitting a gas station. Doesn't seem this way at all around Tula Springs. The North Shore has been pushing folks closer and closer, gas stations and 7-Elevens almost within sight of one another.

Up the street, past the Burdin Diner, is a massive brick building with the largest flag Lou has ever seen. A courthouse perhaps. Or city hall. They usually have clean restrooms. Lou decides it would be wise to make a pit stop, even though the need isn't altogether urgent now. But just in case there is nothing else . . . A preemptive strike.

Luckily, there is diagonal parking. Lou has never been comfortable with parallel. As she pulls in, she wonders why so few civil servants use the free parking here. The place is almost deserted.

But just as she is getting out, she notices the sign. EBENEZER FIRST BAPTIST. SATURDAY: PRO-LIFE BBQ. DOOR PRIZES. SENIOR CITI-

ZENS HALF OFF. WED: REP. GEORGE W. LOT, JR.: KEEP THE CAPITAL IN PUNISHMENT.

With a groan of disgust, Lou wonders what a flag is doing outside a church. And a Confederate flag at that. Looking closer at the limp folds, too heavy to be ruffled by the delicate breeze stirring the crape myrtles, she sees it isn't exactly Confederate. Perhaps it's the Mississippi flag. In any case, she would not use their facilities, even if the doors weren't locked, as they seem to be.

Before pulling away, Lou rearranges the clarinet in the backseat so it's more firmly wedged between the oboe, English horn, sax, and her bassoon. Only five children showed up for her seminar on the family of wind instruments. Even though they were all certified with attention deficit disorder, not one of them fidgeted during Lou's rendition of Ravel's *Bolero* on the bassoon. When Lou finished, these five children presented her with a certificate of appreciation. Their teacher, a Choctaw, offered her a chance to wash up afterward, but Lou declined. Foolishly said, no, thank you. I'm fine.

Though Burdin is barely a town, more like a hamlet languishing beside a single strip mall, Lou can't seem to find the way she came in earlier that morning. It seemed then, after the long drive from Tula Springs, that there was only one main road. No need to look for landmarks to get back home. But as she drives slowly past the diner, she sees there are at least two or three possible choices. If only she could ask directions from someone without having to park and get out. Not a soul is on the sidewalks, though. And little wonder. There isn't a bit of shade to shield the fierce sun. Not a single tree. Anyone seeing a photo might mistake this for Kansas, a ghost town.

After driving for almost an hour with no signs to indicate whether she's going north or south, east or west, toward Meridian (correct), Jackson (less correct, but still O.K.), or Tupelo (very incorrect), Lou wonders if she should turn around, head back to Burdin. She has a map, of course. But she can't find this particular highway on it—1077. The scale is not small enough for a country road.

Lou puts down the map. She has pulled over to the shoulder. It would be a tight squeeze for the BMW, but she might be able to manage to turn around and head back. There's a curve ahead, though. She'll have to be careful, even though she hasn't seen a car in miles.

In reverse, Lou inches toward the gully beside the road. When she shifts, the BMW eases forward gently. But then she hears that awful sound—wheels spinning, trying desperately for a purchase on the edge. Forgetting about the curve ahead, Lou mashes the pedal down. She knows she's only digging herself in deeper, but a tingle of panic keeps her at it. To be stranded out here in the middle of nowhere, night coming on . . . Again and again she floors the pedal, lurching forward herself toward the steering wheel, to give the car some encouragement.

Finally, talking herself down into a more reasonable frame of mind, she gets out to investigate. Joe-pye weed and Queen Anne's lace disguise the real edge of the gully. She has backed up far too close to a perilous drop-off. Much deeper, this gully, than she imagined. The harsh red clay has been eroded twenty feet down, at least.

"Ma'am."

With a gasp, Lou wheels around. A burly man in a John Deere cap looms. Because of the sun, swollen like a star in a drive-in space movie, she cannot see his face. With the slant tangerine rays just behind his squat, apish physique, his features are a blur, unreadable.

Lou edges toward the car door. What a terrible argument she had had with Don just before she left for Mississippi. He had insisted she bring his Smith & Wesson. Keep it in the glove compartment just in case. Don has a thing about Mississippi. He thinks once you cross the state line, people are really different. There's just no telling . . .

Don had won the argument, mainly because Lou was so late. She just didn't have time to reason with him, to let him know how awful she would feel driving through Mississippi with *that* in the glove compartment. But she had to get to Burdin in time. She was

not going to disappoint those children. Each of them was going to
get a chance to blow into a clarinet, an oboe, a bassoon. To hold
the brass, the platinum, the gleaming wood. To feel the real weight
of music, how solid and awkward it could be. Only then could they
appreciate the sound. After knowing what raw, unwieldy matter a
woman struggled with to make her song.

Turning her back on him, Lou manages to sidle into the car,
using the passenger door. Without even having to think, she
presses the automatic lock. Thankfully, all the windows are up.

As she slides over the gearshift, she checks the rearview mirror.
Not there. And he's not in front either.

She has become strangely cool. Rational. She has made up her
mind. If he's white, she'll shoot him. Because Don is right. There
is a limit. She would not be able to endure a violation. Just the
thought of one of those awful rednecks, men who glory in a flag
celebrating the savage enslavement of innocent souls . . . Leering
at her, mocking a body that has fallen, sagged . . . But if he's
African-American, she is equally sure. Yes, rather than be touched,
she will shoot herself. Let him lay a finger on her and . . . Curtains.
Yes, let them come down finally. The end. She has had enough.
More than enough. She is tired, so bone-weary . . .

A rap on the window. She looks. But no one is there. The old
panic is returning. How can he not be there? It's still light enough
to see, isn't it?

Another rap.

Disoriented, she twists, she turns. She's opened the glove compartment. The Smith & Wesson is there, waiting.

Another rap.

*Oh, dear sweet Lord, please spare me this. I don't want to, I don't
want to . . .*

Behind. Quick—behind. Yes, it's the rear window he's rapping
on. But she still can't tell for sure. Black? White? There's that
leathery look smokers have, men who have inhaled three packs a
day for ages. And work in the fields. Dark. Yes, she has seen white
men this dark. But it's not enough. She needs to know for sure.

He's at her window now. She squints, she peers. But still she's not certain. Because there are some rednecks with flattened noses, certain features . . . He's shouting something. A vein is bulging in that horrid bull neck. Bull Conner's . . . Shouting.

Crank her up! Crank her up!

Yes, he must be Caucasian—even though he's dark. She can see how dark he is now, but still . . . Obscene hick. You will not crank me up. Hear? This woman you see has had enough of you and all your Mississippi . . .

Her finger is on the trigger when she catches a glimpse of her. A lithe woman is strolling through a grove of trees. Draped in graceful folds that gather the last rays of the sun, she pauses beside some sort of contraption. The jointed steel, like the remnants of a third-rate museum's T. rex skeleton, hugs a sturdy trunk.

Below the horizon now, the sun powers its slanted rays at the belly of a cumulus. As the burly man in the John Deere cap turns away from the car—yes, Lou has managed to discourage him with the sight of that pistol—she remembers what Don has told her. Light as a cloud? Hardly. This cumulus weighs five hundred tons.

Her heart pounding fiercely, Lou watches him retreat. The dusky man has a peculiar hitch in his stride, one leg a little stiff. It isn't until he's on the other side of the gully, headed toward the grove, that Lou's sense of relief begins to founder. Why, he's headed straight toward *her*, the lady in white. And she doesn't see the danger coming. She's too preoccupied with that contraption, the T. rex.

Lou opens her door. She tries to shout a warning. But nothing will come out. Her throat is too constricted. A warning shot. If she can only manage to give a warning shot into the air. Her finger is on the trigger again. But will the bullet land safely? Where will it go? *I must save her. Help me to overcome these scruples. Help me to shoot, dear Lord! Shoot him, yes him, if he dares lay a hand on her . . .*

He's in the grove now. A strangled shout from Lou makes the lady look away from the tree with the T. rex. She sees now. But instead of fleeing, the lucid folds seem to waft *toward* him, the dusky burly ape.

She takes his paw, holds it to her cheek. Then, a hand on the lady's shoulder, he limps toward the trunk hugged by steel claws.

Back in the car, Lou turns over the engine. With surprising ease, she glides out into the road. He has put something beneath the wheels. Looking out, she catches a glimpse of a palmetto frond. That's why she couldn't see him all this time. He was laboring beneath the car.

Wracked with shame, Lou knows she must get out of the car and head into that grove. Apologize. Let them know what an ass she's been. But then she catches sight of headlights coming around the bend in the road. She simply *can't* stop now to ask for his forgiveness. She doesn't have time to pull over. And there's no room on the shoulder. She could wind up twenty-feet down in the gully.

So she heads off into the night, carrying inside her this terrible need to thank him. As she gathers speed, a strange shudder rocks the air. The T. rex has come to life, grumbling, shaking every last pecan from the hapless tree.

CHAPTER TWENTY-NINE

The doctors, all of them, have forbidden Lou to go. But she is going. If Bill can sneak in and out of the hospital with goulash, Grady with a hound, surely she can steal away for an hour or two.

Mr. Van Buren's memorial service is this morning. It will be at Graceland II, which Burma Van Buren inherited after her husband failed to survive his bypass. Lou is so anxious to see Alpha, who hasn't been to the hospital yet—and Lou is afraid she'll never come. Before it's too late, they will share their burdens. Like sisters, they will talk. This loneliness in Lou that no one else can assuage, surely Alpha will recognize it. Surely it will be healed.

And Alpha is sure to be at Burma's. Lou's heard so much about this mansion from Don. She can't wait to see the parlor with nine velvet sofas. And the fountain with an armed Athena spewing ginger ale from her sword. Lou also craves a glimpse of Burma's mother. Don has told her so many tales about this woman. *Tiny as can be. Almost wouldn't believe she and Burma are related.* As if she were pregnant, Lou yearns for this relish to her bland hospital diet.

With a groan—*Why does it hurt so much? Why can't they say what's wrong with me? Don't ask, don't tell*—Lou lifts an arm to take off her hospital gown. On her last visit, Maigrite brought her the Valentino. It's been so beautifully dry-cleaned, too. And he's never seen her in it, Brother Moodie hasn't. He's going to be officiating at Graceland. In fact, Maigrite said the entire staff at Waist-Watch was invited. Since becoming a multimillionaire, Burma has paid off the TotalPackageMakeOver that her late husband refused to honor.

So this will give Lou a chance to apologize to Brother Moodie for Don's behavior. To prove how much she cares, she's going to enroll in WaistWatch as a client. Get her bod in shape for her new job at St. Jude. Just as soon as the pain subsides. She's been in this darn room long enough. A change of scene, that's what she needs. How long can she be expected to live with a television going twenty-four hours a day?

Lou carefully removes the IV. Maigrite's provided her with a flesh-colored Band-Aid. No one will even see the little scars from the needles.

Once Lou is in the Valentino, she wonders what could be wrong. Why is it hanging on her so funny? So big. She peers down, examines it. Yes, it is hers. That corn-dog stain from Don's former boss's aunt, there's a faint penumbra that no dry cleaner could ever get out. But did someone let out the waist? Even the shoulders seem to droop.

Well, nowadays drooping is stylish. Look at Bill, the way he dresses.

And look, the shoes fit. Almost. A little roomy, that's all. More comfortable this way.

The phone rings. It's Don, calling from work. Yes, he's got a job. The long wait has paid off. He's working for GinKo Pharmaceuticals in Ozone. They're developing a prescription sleep aid from a tree found only in the upper Amazon. It's also supposed to strengthen your bones.

Twice a day, without fail, Don visits her at the hospital. Before and after work. It's a terrible strain for him, since he's bought a house in Ozone, right on Lake Pontchartrain. Not far from GinKo. Don's taken some snapshots to show her. It's as old as the house on Coffee Ridge. There's a gallery, too, just like Grady's. Don's bought rockers for it, antique oak rockers from a bankrupt marquis's castle on eBay. They'll look out over the lake at dusk, she and Don, with a drink to ease them into night. Before Don had moved into the house, he had tried to get her transferred to St. Jude General in Ozone. But he had discovered that even his GinKo insurance would only cover Lou if she remained at Pentecostal in Tula Springs. In any case, she's trying to get him to cut down the visits from twice to once a day. Arriving at the office exhausted every day will not be good for her darling boy.

Yes, my love, Lou says into the receiver. *Why is this phone so heavy? Do all hospital phones weigh a ton?* Yes, I'm fine. No, no, Don. Don't come by this evening. Please, do me a favor. Take a break today. I really don't feel like a visit this evening. I've got a test, they're taking me downstairs for a test this afternoon. And you know those sedatives. I'll be out cold. I don't want you to barge in, darling, and wake me up.

Yes, yes, I'm sure, Don. I really mean it. Go home and make yourself a nice Gibson, dear. Yes, yes, darling, soon. Soon I'll be with you on the porch. No, please don't carve my name on the rocker, Donnie. What will people think? You're just too crazy, little man. Too crazy for me. Yes, yes . . . Soon. It won't be long.

"Lou, Lou?"

The gentle hand shakes her awake. Slumped over in the turquoise chair, Lou feels a smile lighting up her entire body. *You've come. Oh, Mrs. Ompala. I'm so ashamed. I've been meaning to visit you. But my allergy, I just can't be near gazelles. Is it good for you there? Are you happy? Do you like the giraffe?*

"Lou, Lou . . ."

I'll help you find your child, dear woman. I know how hard it must be to wander all over creation, searching for an end to that pain, that guilt . . . Alpha will help us find the child . . .

"It's late, Lou . . ."

Yes, I know. I should have thanked your husband long ago. I've been hoping for a chance to apologize, to thank him for getting me out of that rut. Isn't it funny, dear, it turns out I've known you all along, even before we met . . .

"Come on, Lou. Wake up."

Lou takes the lace hankie Maigrite offers. She rubs her eyes. "Oh, it's you. Maigrite. Oh, my . . . You're . . ."

"What's wrong, Lou? What's the matter?"

Lou stares, a little lost. It's like being in a museum, the chill, the hush of great art. For Mrs. Pickens seems almost too stately. Her beauty is sobering. What Lou remembers of Maigrite in the office is only a fitful parody of the reality here before her now. The olive skin seems to glow with the cool sensuality of an Athena.

"What have you done to yourself, Maigrite?"

"I *told* Burma that bacon diet was no good. Had to buy myself a whole new wardrobe, you know."

"No, no, I mean you're . . . stunning."

"Oh, come off it. I'm nothing but a little pig. Had to take my watch to the jeweler just so I could get it over my wrist."

"Mr. Pickens is a lucky man."

"I catch him giving Burma any strange looks tonight, mooning over her, he's going to see that luck change right fast. Oh, Lou, careful, honey," Maigrite adds as she helps Lou out of the turquoise chair.

Lou feels a little dizzy standing up. But this is only natural. She's been in bed so long. Long enough for Maigrite's harsh, angular features to mellow.

"I don't know how you talked me into this, Lou. It's crazy. Don will kill me if he finds out I let you go to Burma's."

"Don't worry about him. He's not coming by tonight. I told him . . ."

"And the nurses. How're we supposed to sneak by them?"

"That's the last thing to worry about. All you have to do is ring for them and you can be sure they'll never show up." Lou presses the hefty call button by her headboard.

"Oh, Lou, honey, stop! Oh, careful!"

Lou's heel has broken off. Or so it seems. After Maigrite has caught her in her arms, Lou sees that it's only her ankles. They've given way after so many weeks in bed.

"That's all it is, Maigrite. Weak ankles. I'll be fine."

"I don't know, Lou. Maybe we should wait till some other time. You were talking so strange when I came in . . ."

"No, Maigrite. Please, darling, don't . . ."

"I never should've let you talk me into this. What if . . ."

"Maigrite, just five minutes. Give me five minutes there. I won't stay long. I want to see Burma's house. And Alpha. There's something I got to tell Alpha."

"I'll get Alpha to come by tomorrow. During visiting hours."

"No, no, it'll be too late. It's got to be now. Tonight. Right now."

"Don't be such a child, Lou. There's plenty of time to . . . Oh!"

Lou's other ankle has given out. Gently, she seems wafted to the bed.

"Now you listen to me, Lou. Enough nonsense. I'm going to get a doctor. You're in no condition to . . ."

"No, Maigrite. Please. The doctors won't let me go. I've got to get out. I've got to see Alpha before . . ."

In her red Valentino, Lou half lies, half sits on the adjustable bed. Maigrite has hurried out of the room, her gold lamé gown crackling and swishing like leaves in a stiff autumn wind.

Lou clutches the ermine cape Maigrite, in her haste, has left behind. It's a gift from Burma. Genuine ermine.

Would you like to have a cup of coffee with me? Let's sit down for a few minutes. Have a little chat. You don't need to vacuum any more. I'll do the rest if . . . Please, just one cup, that's all. Oh, heavenly days, I know you're busy, but . . .

A tender ache soothes the precious fur. How long it seems, that hall. Will she ever be able to make it all that way? Someone please . . .

Come, sweet Alpha. Come.